Heroes and Hounds

HEROES *and* HOUNDS

BY BILL MILLER

Illustrated by Mary Burkhardt

With love!
Mary

ISBN 1456310364
EAN 9781456310363

Designed by Al Burkhardt

This book is dedicated to Mrs. Jane Sheldon, *former Master of Foxhounds for the Norfolk Hunt. It was her story of a missing hound that inspired* Heroes and Hounds *and the book was originally written as a present for her. Thank you Jane for the inspiration and for the many years we rode the trail together. Hampton also sends special dog kisses just for you.*

SPECIAL THANKS

I would like to express extreme thanks and deep appreciation to my wife, Lynne, who spent countless hours reading and editing this manuscript. Without her help this jumble of words would never have made it onto the printed page in such exquisite form. She kept the clichés out and the story flowing.

Heroes and Hounds

CHAPTER 1

From the living room window she could see forever. Past the oak tree with the tire swing. Past the vegetable garden where the large green pumpkins were turning Halloween orange. Past the barn with the hay stacked to the rafters for the coming winter. Out into the rolling Virginia hills where the amber grasses of autumn touched the gray skies on this threatening morning.

Carly balanced on her tiptoes, her nose barely touching the frosty windowpane. Eleven years old, she stood exactly four feet tall. What she lacked in size, she made up for in her enthusiasm for life. Carly was a bonfire of energy and was wildly curious about everything. Her heart was as big as the surrounding valley that she loved to explore. Each day brought the promise of adventure and Carly was always eager to take on a challenge, despite any dangers that might be waiting on a new or unknown trail.

This morning as she watched from the living room window, a light mist fell outside, leaving a gleam on the fence and porch rails. Her breath added frost on the window, her eyes wide with anticipation. In the kitchen her grandfather lowered the heat on the skillet where pancakes were turning golden brown. Carly lived with her grandfather on his 200-acre farm. Grandpa Oakley was a burly man. A shock of gray hair showed no signs of thinning. His face was etched with wrinkles from too many days of sitting in the sun on his John Deere tractor. He hummed a tune from another era. The 'Olden Days' as Carly liked to joke, back when television was black and white. Even though Grandpa Oakley was seventy-years-old, he was as strong as his prize bull Samson and often proved it at the county fair wrestling championships, beating men half his age.

The smell from the kitchen drifted across the living room where Buster the gray tomcat sniffed the air and purred. He loved pancakes with maple syrup. Grandpa Oakley complained that the cat was too fat and wouldn't catch mice if Carly kept feeding him scraps from the table. Carly always looked sad when her grandfather said this. He said it at every meal but didn't really mean it. So Buster kept eating human food and getting fat. And the mice had the run of the barn. Carly liked the mice and all the animals at the farm. Even the red fox that came to visit at dusk.

Grandpa said the fox was spying on the chickens, plotting and scheming, waiting for a dark, moonless night when he'd return and make a feast of the hens. In the two years Carly had been living at the farm, no hens or roosters had disappeared, except the ones Grandpa selected for supper. So Carly and the fox became good friends. Sort of. While they shared a common space, the fox always kept his distance and Carly kept hers. From time to time, Carly saw the fox smile back when she smiled at him. At least she thought she did.

"Carly!" Grandpa called again. Buster sat up ready to

spring into action. But Carly didn't move from the window. It wouldn't be long now. She heard them before she saw them coming. They were still in the shadow of the hill. At first it was a low, distinct sound. The chorus of two-dozen hounds yelping in a feverish pitch. As the hounds got closer, Carly could hear the hammer of horses' hooves in close pursuit followed by the mellow tones of a brass horn blaring out its shrill call. Carly, ignoring her grandfather and the awaiting pancakes, dashed out the screen door onto the front porch for a closer look. The mist had turned into a steady rain, forming small puddles beneath the downspouts along the edge of the porch. From this new vantage point, she could see the pack of hounds running and bounding through the tall brown grass. They followed the fox scent over a wild course, now going straight, now cutting left, now doubling back. The hounds darted and dashed at each twist in the path. Carly watched in awe.

Then came the horses, prancing and snorting, their coats glistening with rain, steam rising from their backs. On the galloping steeds rode the finely dressed ladies and gentlemen of the Riverdale Hunt Club. Leading the way was the Master of Foxhounds, Thurston Drury, wearing a black riding cap, a long scarlet riding coat with bright brass buttons, a yellow vest, white riding britches and tall black boots with tan tops. Silver spurs, a hand whip, and a brass horn completed his wardrobe. His silver-gray horse, nostrils flaring, kicked soft sod high into the air, as it galloped across the open field. Forty other smartly turned-out members of the Hunt followed the Master.

Several times each Fall on Saturday mornings, the Hunt would come through Grandpa Oakley's farm. In preparation, he took down barbed wire and electric fences, put the sheep and cows in a back pasture, and opened part of his two hundred acres to the Hunt. There was a mutual understanding between the farmers of the valley and the members of the Hunt. It was the job of the Hunt to keep the fox population under control. In return, the farmers graciously opened their vast tracts of land for the equestrian sport. Carly treasured these Saturday mornings. Farm life could get very lonely and she loved any kind of excitement.

As Carly watched the riders thunder by, her imagination swept her into the middle of the hunt field, riding a fiery young thoroughbred horse. The wind whistled by her ears, the rain pelted her face. Her heart beat wildly as her horse galloped down the side of one hill and charged up another. She could feel her muscles tighten as she focused on a fast approaching, menacing, four-foot stone wall. She held her breath as the horse in front of her jumped the obstacle. Now it was her turn. She pressed her legs tighter around her horse's girth, urging him forward. Without missing a stride, her horse soared into the air, sailing over the large stone wall, as if in slow motion. Her daydream carried her into a grassy field where she raced across an open meadow.

"Carly!" her grandfather shouted impatiently from the doorway. His voice startled Carly back into reality.

"Wait a while, grandpa!" she sputtered, her breath coming in short bursts.

"Pancakes are getting cold and besides Buster is having a

fit waiting. You know if you keep feeding him scraps, he's never going to catch any mice. Dang 'ole cat just sleeps and eats, sleeps and eats," he said, joining her on the porch.

Carly smiled at her grandfather, as they watched the last riders splash through a shallow stream before disappearing into a stand of river birch trees.

"Fine looking group," he observed.

"Someday I'm going to ride with them. Like the wind, Grandpa," said Carly.

"What's that you say?" asked Grandpa Oakley.

"Oh, nothing. Boy, those pancakes smell great," she said, changing the subject. She whistled to Buster who was already walking in and out and around her legs as she headed into the kitchen.

CHAPTER 2

The hounds pranced and yelped as they cut a path through the wet grass. At the head of the pack was Snoot, a veteran hound with clearly defined markings of black, tan, and white. He was sturdy with springy legs and a strong back. The way he carried himself over the countryside revealed his many years of hunting experience. He was proud to be out front. Following Snoot were nearly two dozen other hounds, some all white with only a few dashes of tan or black mixed in. Some were nearly all tan with only a few lonely white patches showing through. The hounds had names like Jasmine, Horatio, Tinker, and Annabelle.

Toward the rear of the pack was Hampton, a yearling hound on his first Saturday hunt. As he was growing up, he had been allowed to go on schooling walks with the older hounds, and, once, just before the hunting season opened, he had participated in a short weekday hunt called a cubbing. He

had behaved so well that today Mr. Drury selected him as a replacement for one of the older hounds that had hurt a paw and couldn't run. Hampton didn't mind being a last minute pick, a substitute for a more experienced hound. In fact, before leaving the kennel, he paraded vainly in front of the other rookies who were being left behind. He was a quick learner and if he just followed the hound in front of him, he thought, everything would turn out fine.

The first few miles had been terrific for Hampton. The light mist felt good against his coat and he loved the grasses swishing by his long, floppy ears. He ran with his nose inches off the ground, sorting through hundreds of scents that clung to wet leaves or hung just above the ground. Scent of deer, possum, and cows. Birds and horses. Even human smells. His keen mind picked through the potpourri of smells, discarding the ones he thought useless on this day. One scent was clearly stronger than the others. Another he could distinctly remember from the few times he had run with the pack. Fox! Something in the back of his mind told him this was the scent he was to follow. It was strong and full and easy to detect, and it was luring him along a line as straight as an arrow.

Suddenly the line of the scent took a sharp right turn and Hampton, in mad pursuit, made a hairpin turn, his four legs scrambling to keep from tumbling head over heels. Then the scent doubled back. At first, Hampton didn't know what had happened to it. It just stopped. He stopped, too, pushed his nose close to the ground and flung his snout upward toward the sky. Confused, he tried crying out like the other hounds. But what came out was a broken, shrill yelp that startled even Hampton. He was embarrassed and thought better of speaking again. In the next instant, Chadwick, a fine young two-year-old who was a regular with the pack, pranced past Hampton and scampered down the trail in the direction from which they had come. Hampton whirled around, doing a 180-degree turn and followed closely on the heels of the experienced older hound. Six or seven other panting hounds flanked Hampton on his right and left.

There were two other sharp turns before the scent straightened out, following a course over a stone wall, past a stand of apple trees, and through a small brook where large rocks formed a little bridge. Hampton was tired. This was more running than he had ever done and the excitement added to his thirst. The little brook was very inviting and Hampton didn't see any harm in sneaking a quick drink. He had been working very hard and deserved a little rest. The water felt good as he stepped into the streambed. He worked diligently lapping up the water at a pace exceeding that of his rapidly beating heart. It felt so good, Hampton decided to cool off his entire body and thought nothing of lying down right in the middle of the stream. It was something he often did back in the kennel, where a brook splashed through the middle of the hounds' exercise field.

Hampton lay there for a dreamy minute or two, all thoughts of the hunt and the other hounds far from his mind. Perhaps it was the rotted tree branch cracking and falling to the ground that snapped Hampton's mind back to the task at hand. His head turned frantically in all directions, searching for the other hounds. In desperation, he leaped higher and higher into the air to see over the tall grass. His nose bounced off the ground as he searched for the familiar scent. He turned left, then right, then doubled back over the stream, alternately looking and sniffing. Hampton stopped in a small clearing at the top of a hill where he could look out over the fields. The rain fell faster and harder making it difficult for him to see. He tried to find any trace of the once strong fox scent he had been following, but an itch needed immediate attention. After a quick pause to scratch it, he paced the grassy knoll looking and smelling.

Now he was getting nervous. There were no familiar smells. No sights he recognized. Hampton realized he was alone. Left behind. The Hunt had gone off without him.

Hampton knew his legs were young and strong, capable of making up the growing distance between him and the horses and hounds. If only he knew in what direction they had gone. From where Hampton stood, the valleys and hills stretched out in all directions, as far as his eyes could see. All he could do was pick one path and hope his instinct was right. He looked west one more time and, after some thought, decided to go east, where a tractor road led through a gate and into a thick forest. It seemed like a good choice at the time. The rain fell at a steady rate, the wind picked up, and Hampton, cold and scared, set off to find the pack.

CHAPTER 3

The fire her grandfather built in the woodstove crackled and popped and its radiating heat made Buster the cat especially happy. He purred as he slept on the floor near the warm glow. Carly sat on her heels a few steps away. The rain beat a steady rhythm on the roof as Carly carefully cleaned her pony's bridle. The tack had been a present for her eleventh birthday two months earlier and her grandfather had told her it would last a lifetime if she kept it cleaned and oiled. Carly was proud of the bridle and loved the way it framed her pony's pale, white face. If it stopped raining in time, Carly would take the pony for a long, Saturday afternoon hack into the woods. When the sun came out, Carly would be ready to go.

Grandpa Oakley was in the barn working on his aging John Deere tractor. The old man treated the tractor like a member of the family. Cleaning it, polishing it. Keeping it shiny, like new. Looking at the tractor, no one could tell it was more than a dozen years old, faithfully harvesting fields, cutting hay, moving rocks, and even plowing snow on bitter winter mornings for the elderly farmer. Half a dozen cows wandered in to get out of the rain and to check out what was keeping the farmer busy. Carly's pony watched her grandfather from his square box stall twenty feet away. He dined on his lunch of timothy hay and watched the activity as he chewed. Carly's pony was dapple-gray, measuring almost thirteen hands just a little taller than Carly. His name was Monroe. Carly thought Monroe was a funny name for a pony, but he had come with the name and it had grown on Grandpa Oakley and his granddaughter. Monroe was Monroe and any thoughts of changing his name were long forgotten.

Every once in a while, Carly heard Grandpa turn the tractor on, run it for a few minutes, then turn it off again. Grandpa told Carly he would teach her all about tractors and engines and stuff like that and Carly told him she really wanted to learn about tractors and machines. But she never seemed to have the time. She was learning all she could about horses and riding. Combined with all the subjects she was learning in the fifth grade, tractors and engines and stuff like that would have to wait.

The engine purred, and so did Buster, having done a good job finishing the leftover pancakes. All that food had made

Carly's feline friend very tired, forcing him to take a nap perched on the windowsill. He didn't budge when a shadow flashed across the barnyard. From the barn Grandpa Oakley didn't see it either. Out of the corner of her eye, Carly thought she saw something dart by. She wasn't sure what it was. Perhaps it was a fox, or a bird flying low to the ground. Carly put down the bridle and stepped to the window. Whatever it

was, if in fact it was anything at all, had already passed out of view. A slight ripple in the large puddle, which had formed between the house and barn, was the only visible evidence that something had moved across the yard. What had caused the ripple, Carly did not know. Many creatures, large and small, passed through the farm every day. Some on wing, some on foot. Some friendly, others too timid to pause to say hello.

She hesitated only a minute at the window, and then returned to cleaning her bridle. Her thoughts were of riding her pony later that day and with the hunt some day. The tractor hummed in the distance and Buster opened one eye, yawned, and returned to his catnap, confident he hadn't missed anything important. In the distance the lonely whistle of a railroad locomotive hauling freight cars echoed in the wind.

CHAPTER 4

Mr. Drury, the hunt Master, urged his horse forward up a steep incline. He was drenched from head to foot, water dripping off the front lip of his velvet hunt cap. The scarlet, heavy melton coat kept his body dry where it covered him, but his pants, gloves, and leather boots were soaked. The belly and legs of his horse were covered with dark blotches of thick mud, along with the stirrups and leather girth that held the

German jumping saddle tightly in place. Every time the horse exhaled, his breath was visible, as the hot air exploded into the cold, damp day. His sides heaved with each breath. Steam rose off his back.

Sitting deep in the saddle, Mr. Drury pulled back on the reins and brought his mount to a halt. He yelled a command at the hounds calling them off the scent. Quickly and obediently nineteen panting foxhounds returned to the Master's side. He patted his horse's neck and paid tribute to the lead hound for obeying so quickly. Their reward would be a long drink in the pond next to a clearing where the hunt had stopped for a rest. Several of the whippers-in, the riders who help the Master control and contain the hounds, were on alert should any of the hounds cross the invisible line which had been established between the pond and the hunt field. Mr. Drury counted the hounds for a second time and the number was coming out the same, nine and one-half couples. Hounds are counted as pairs and the hunt had started with ten couples, or twenty hounds. It was clear that one was missing. The Master asked Sharon Tidefield, a seasoned whipper-in, to take her own count, but the results were the same, nineteen hounds.

Mr. Drury ran the names of the hounds through his head at computer speed and he quickly knew which of the hounds had not made it through to this checkpoint. It was Hampton, the young hound, whose name had been added to the list at the last minute. The Master snapped orders to the staff members, and before he finished the sentence two of his whips were flying back across the field in search of the missing

hound. There was a buzz in the field as word of the missing hound passed from member to member. Mr. Drury called the hounds, most of whom were lying in the pond, lapping water from a prone position. The hounds obeyed, some quicker than others, and without delay the pack was walking in stride twenty feet in front of the Master's horse.

The other riders assumed their positions in the field, guided by an unwritten roster, which everyone knew and followed. In less than thirty seconds the hounds were on the scent again and the entire hunt rocketed across the Virginia countryside, leaving hoof prints in the soggy earth and a wake in every stream they crossed. An hour later, the two whips in search of Hampton reported back that they hadn't found a trace of the missing hound. An all out search by foot, horseback, and automobile was launched later that day, after the traditional hunt tea.

CHAPTER 5

Hampton was cold and tired. He had run for miles and miles. Sometimes in a straight line. Sometimes in circles. No matter how far or how fast he ran he seemed to get nowhere. At least nowhere that he could recognize. All the fields and streams, bushes, trees, and hills looked the same. And none of the smells he followed along the way led him where he wanted so badly to go. Home. How nice it would be to sleep in his own kennel. Dry and warm. There was comfort in the company of the other hounds. A meal and fresh water would be waiting for him. For now, that seemed a lifetime away as Hampton loped down a fresh trail.

As he moved along, he noticed something was different. The landscape was changing. He was confused by sights and sounds he hadn't seen or heard during his short time on Earth. The soft grass of the meadows turned into hard cement. Where the tall trees once stood there were houses and stores. Buildings of all shapes, sizes and colors. And there were cars. Lots of cars. Humans scurried about. Some carried umbrellas. Others ran through the rain. No one noticed the cold, wet, lost hound. If they did, no one stopped. No one asked if he needed help. No one offered him a warm place to rest or supper.

Hampton was in a place he'd never seen before. Never even dreamed that such a place could exist. Frightened, he carried his tail between his hind legs, but like a good hound, he pushed his head low to the ground, in the event a familiar scent presented itself. He ran for a few feet, then stopped and looked around. Trees, garbage cans, and parked cars were good places to hide, darting along only when it seemed safe. Hampton tensed each time a car raced by on the street leaving a trail of wet tire marks and blue smoke that lingered for a few seconds before evaporating into the air. He didn't like automobile smoke. It made his eyes itchy.

Hampton crouched low beside the tire of a parked car fearful of the speeding automobiles and trucks. A yellow van with a loud radio splashed through a puddle near the curb spraying oily water over the hound. He tried shaking the oily wetness from his coat, but by now he was drenched. His small body shivered in the cold and his tail hung low to the ground as he awaited a break in the traffic. Beams from the headlights of passing cars danced through the fog as night blackened the day. The wet pavement magnified the oncoming headlights temporarily blinding Hampton.

Turning his head away, he sat on a curb for what seemed like hours until the last of the hissing tires faded into the distance. Soon the only light was from an overhead street lamp that flickered in the rain. He thought it would be safe to cross now and slowly walked out into the street. But he was wrong.

The wind blew rain into his face and he was temporarily blinded again. And with the wind howling, he didn't hear the fancy sports car as it squealed around the corner. The headlights bore down on him. Now he wanted to run, to spin around and dart under a parked car. Back to safety. But he stood paralyzed, the sports car almost upon him. The sound was deafening. His mind said run, but the signals never reached the muscles in his legs.

At the last moment, the driver saw Hampton frozen in the street. He frantically spun the steering wheel hard to the left and the sports car swerved sharply, grazing Hampton's left front paw, enough to injure the hound. The driver did not stop, and, as the music from his car radio faded into the night,

Hampton felt the pain growing in his leg, radiating from the injured paw and racing through his body into the nerve center of his brain.

Hampton knew he was hurt but didn't know how badly. The lost hound tried putting weight on the injured leg, but the pain told him this wasn't a good idea. He limped away carefully keeping the injured paw off the hard ground. He wouldn't try crossing the roadway again. Instead, he hobbled slowly down the sidewalk. The street was deserted now. Only an occasional car or truck passed. All the stores were closed and there were no people around who could help the injured hound as he made his way along the lonely street. The brick buildings, small stores, and shops turned into houses and barns as Hampton wandered away from the town. The distances between houses grew farther and farther apart. He was still too shaken to try crossing the street. Why he wanted to cross the street in the first place was not clear to Hampton. While his thoughts were fuzzy, something deep inside his brain was telling him to head north. North meant crossing the street. It was Hampton's built-in direction finder, passed down through hundreds of generations of fine hunting dogs. But the pain in his leg told him to disregard his inner voice.

After a brief rest, Hampton hobbled on three legs toward a steep embankment where the pavement ended and the rain had turned the dirt into thick mud. The hound misjudged his distance from the edge of the hill and, before he knew it, he was tumbling down the steep slope. He landed on his back, his tan and black coat covered with the reddish-brown Virginia mud. It was then his luck turned around. At the bottom of the hill was a large, cylindrical, cement culvert, part of a new sewer system being installed in the roadway above. It was large enough for Hampton to crawl in and be protected from the rain. At the head of the cement tube was a puddle of thick mud. Hampton settled into the shelter with his injured paw dangling over the edge into the puddle. As it dried the mud formed a natural cast around the sore leg providing welcome relief. He was still hungry, but it was warm in the culvert and he was drying off. Tomorrow when his leg felt better, Hampton would find food and then continue his journey home. The rain fell with a steady beat on the roof of his tiny shelter. The patter of the raindrops was soothing and Hampton soon fell asleep. He was a very tired puppy and it had been a long and dramatic day.

CHAPTER 6

Shortly after dark, a loud rapping at the front door echoed throughout the wood frame of the Oakley farmhouse. Carly heard the banging from the kitchen where she was drying the dinner dishes, putting them in the cupboard to the left of the sink. She stood on a small stool to reach the shelf. Buster heard the banging from his perch on the kitchen table where he had fallen asleep convinced he had consumed every morsel of leftover food. Grandpa Oakley heard the banging in the living room where he was sitting in his large recliner reading the newspaper. He raised his glasses, put down the paper, and walked to the door. Carly looked over her shoulder, through the hallway and into the living room. Buster opened one eye, saw that food was not being offered, and resumed his dream. The rain beat heavily on the roof and a bolt of lighting sizzled across the night sky lighting the earth for miles around.

As the front door slowly opened, the light from Grandpa's reading lamp revealed a very tall, thin man, dressed in a long, canvas raincoat with a full-brimmed rain hat. Water droplets fell from the brim making pinging sounds on the wooden porch. His face reflected many years of outdoor activities. His eyes were deeply set, and this evening there was trouble etched in his brow. Grandpa recognized the man immediately and thrust a warm, dry hand toward him in friendly greeting. It was Thurston Drury, Master of the Hunt.

Grandpa's voice was friendly as he greeted the visitor, "Good evening, Thurston. What brings you out on such a miserable night."

"Evening, Mather, mind if I come in and dry off?"

"Of course, Thurston," Grandpa Oakley said. "Come in. Come in."

Thurston Drury wiped his boots on the mat outside the door, took off his cap and raincoat and left them to dry on the covered porch. He was still wearing his riding britches, boots and white, collarless shirt. A blue denim jacket replaced his scarlet riding coat. Silently, Carly left the kitchen stool and, half-hidden by his baggy overalls, stood behind her Grandfather. She looked up at the tall man whose face bore the wetness of the night.

"Cup of coffee, Thurston?" Grandpa Oakley inquired.

"Aren't you kind. It's been quite a day."

Carly eyes couldn't hide her excitement. It wasn't every day that such an important member of the equestrian community paid a visit. She had never really met the Master, although he had waved at her several times as she watched the Hunt go by in the backfields. And once she had seen him in town, as she ate an ice cream cone with her grandfather. But she had been too shy to do much more than just nod and smile at the gentleman who rode with such style and grace. Now he was in her house not more than five feet away.

"Good evening, Carly," Mr. Drury said, noticing the child who was watching him from the safety of her grandfather's shadow.

"Hello, Mr. Drury." Carly answered, the words barely bridging the gap between them. As she spoke, Carly smiled in disbelief that Mr. Drury knew her name. She thought that she had always been invisible in his presence.

Grandpa Oakley returned from the kitchen carrying a large mug of steaming coffee. He set it on the coffee table in front of the aging couch and motioned to Mr. Drury to sit down. He moved with grace for such a large man as he settled into the soft pillows, unconcerned with the gray cat hairs that were sprinkled over the upholstery. A gift from Buster. Grandpa sat in his large recliner, pushing the neck of the reading lamp toward the fireplace, so that he would have an unobstructed view of his guest. Carly stood behind her grandfather's chair, barely visible over its large, swooping back. She was eager to learn why Mr. Drury was out on such a cold, wet night. She knew he couldn't be here on just a social call. Mr. Drury sipped from the coffee mug, enjoying the warmth it brought to his lips. He did not speak for several minutes. Grandpa Oakley, schooled in the rituals of country etiquette, waited for his guest to open the conversation. Carly balanced on her right foot, then her left foot, then back to the right.

Mr. Drury spoke in a deep baritone. He came right to the point. "One of the hounds is missing. Young one named Hampton. Just over a year old. We think he left the pack at the rise beyond your farm and I was wondering whether you saw him come through here?"

"We saw the hounds and horses come through just before ten this morning," Grandpa offered. "It was raining pretty hard."

"You're telling me," said the Master. "I think I've been wet all day."

"I didn't see any stray dog.... uh, hound," Grandpa replied, catching himself. He knew it was not proper etiquette to refer to a working foxhound as a dog. Carly smiled behind the recliner, out of sight of the Master. Mr. Drury was too concerned with the missing hound to notice the slip. "I was out in the barn all day working on that gosh darn tractor. Could've slipped in the barn while I wasn't looking, but I didn't see or hear anything unusual. I'll take a real good look at first light tomorrow morning."

"How about you, Carly?" asked the Master.

"There! He said my name again," Carly thought to herself. She slowly came out from the back of the recliner and into the light, which cast a sharp shadow across her face. Her auburn hair was curled and frizzy from the damp weather.

"No sir, I didn't see any strange animals, here, sir," she said shyly. "But I'll look all around tomorrow."

"Good, good, good. We can use your help. We've had a dozen people out looking since the end of the Hunt. No sign

anywhere. But in this weather tracks don't keep very well. Hate to lose such a fine prospect as Hampton."

Mr. Drury drank the last of his coffee and set the cup down on a corner of the coffee table, where the fire reflected in its mirror-like surface. "How's that pony of yours, young lady?"

"My pony?" asked Carly, shocked that he knew she had a pony.

"Yes, Carly. What's his name?"

"Monroe," Carly said proudly.

"Monroe, yes, Monroe. I always liked that little pony. I remember when Bitsy Jackson rode that pony in the Hunt. What a great little jumper. And you couldn't beat its spirit. That pony could keep up with all the big thoroughbreds."

Carly beamed. She had never been told that her pony had once run with the other horses and foxhounds. Monroe was already at the farm when Carly came to live with her grandfather two years ago.

"He can still fly like the wind," Carly replied, her shyness evaporating.

"I'll bet he can," Mr. Drury replied as he stood to leave. "Now don't forget. Keep a sharp eye out for Hampton, the missing hound."

Carly did not hear his parting words. Her thoughts were of her pony and once again she was riding across the fields of Virginia. She never heard Mr. Drury walk out the door, and, as he drove down the long winding driveway, the lights of his Land Rover were lost in her dreams.

"They're not the brightest dogs," her grandfather said not caring that he didn't refer to them as hounds.

"What's that?" Carly asked.

"Never mind," her grandfather growled. "Tomorrow we'll take a look around. Got too much work around this farm to be bothered looking for a lost mutt."

"I'll find the missing hound," Carly stated matter-of-factly. In her mind she was replaying the scene that happened earlier in the afternoon while her grandfather was working on his tractor. Carly had seen something odd dash across the barnyard. Caught a glimpse of it. "Could it have been black and tan and white?" she asked herself. But it was just a blur in the rain, and she couldn't tell for sure if it had been Hampton, or any hound or dog for that matter.

"I'm sure you will, sweetheart," Grandpa replied. He picked up his newspaper and continued reading about how dangerous the cities were getting.

Carly picked up Buster and stroked his back. The gray cat yawned and smiled, as he looked lovingly at Carly. She closed her eyes, as her hand caressed the soft, furry ball on her knee. Buster purred as thunder echoed in the hills.

CHAPTER 7

The sun was fiery red as it came up over the hill spreading welcome daylight throughout the valley. It reflected off a puddle and right into the sleeping face of Hampton who had holed up in the cement tube for the night. He slowly opened one eye. Then the other. He sniffed the air, drinking in the smells of a new October day. It was the sweet smell that lingers after a heavy rainfall. The sun was out, but the air was still heavy, leaving fog in the valley and steam rising from golden, wet leaves, which in a few days would say good-bye to their summer branches and float down to Earth. The sunlight cut beams through the changing autumn trees making the vivid colors even more vibrant.

Hampton licked his leg. It was stiff from the mud that had hardened into a rather effective cast. The hound balanced on three legs, not yet trusting his injured leg to bear any weight. Slowly Hampton shifted his balance to test the pain level. To his surprise, the leg felt pretty good. The hairs of his coat were dry and stiff, sticking out at funny angles. Hampton didn't care much about the way he looked. He wanted to get home. And he couldn't believe how hungry he was.

He lifted his nose to the air and picked up the most powerful smell he had ever experienced. It almost knocked him over which wouldn't have been hard to do in Hampton's condition. He trotted off in the direction of the smell that hovered just above his outstretched nose. He thought this odd, having been trained to follow scents much closer to the ground. Hampton knew this might lead to a meal. Often in the evening back at the kennel, strong odors wafted over the exercise yards. He never could figure just what these smells meant, but somehow he thought food might be involved. Most good scents led to a reward at the end of the run. Hampton hoped the reward at the end of this run would be breakfast. He followed the scent as it drifted down a dirt road. The scent got stronger and stronger. Hampton crossed a small creek and limped up a hill where a rusted, worn out, battered house trailer sat in a small clearing. Over the years, the paint had cracked and faded and rust bullied its way across the metal sides. Many years ago, the house trailer had been painted rainbow colors, which swirled and danced across the roof and sides. At one time it must have been the pride and joy of the Woodstock generation. Now it sat as a decaying monument to a forgotten era. Something inside smelled good to Hampton.

Without hesitation, he walked right up to the patched screen door and tried looking inside. It was dark except for the dim glow from a bare light bulb hanging from the ceiling. At a kitchen table sat a shadowy figure, a broken man. Long hair, long beard. Hampton couldn't make out any details. The person inside focused on a small, portable, black and white television that flickered on the table in front of him. Hampton stared at the figure for what seemed a long time. But the person didn't blink from the television tube. Hampton grew very tired of this waiting game. At the kennel, he was fed at precisely the same time every day. No waiting. Hampton couldn't take it any more. The first sound that came out of his mouth was a little squeak. Then Hampton startled even himself with a long, loud howl that could be heard for miles. The man at the table jumped a few inches out of his chair, turned his face toward the door and peered at Hampton through red, bloodshot eyes. His voice was gravelly and low. As he spoke, the "s" sounds at the end his words whistled through missing teeth. His clothes were torn and dirty, and it looked like he hadn't had a bath in a year. There was a distinct odor about the man, but it wasn't as sweet or as powerful as the scent that brought Hampton to this wretched place.

Hampton sat down wagging his tail. He had been discovered. His front feet shuffled in anticipation. He could almost taste the food in his mouth. Hampton didn't know what a shotgun was. He had never seen one.

So there was no reason for Hampton to fear the long-barreled, 20-gauge shotgun that Strange Willie, the man who occupied the trailer, now held in his hands. A tall man, he was forced to stoop as he walked, his head almost touching the ceiling. Hampton wiggled and wagged. Slowly Strange Willie's eyes focused on the foxhound sitting on his front step.

"Well, well, well," Strange Willie spoke aloud, "whatta we got here?

He spoke in slow, slurred syllables. Each word bounced off the roof of his mouth as he chattered.

Hampton wagged and barked. For all he knew, Strange Willie would be his new best friend.

"Whoa," Strange Willie said in a startled tone. "It's one of them fancy, dancy, hunting dawgs what hangs around with rich folk. What'ye doin' around here, pal. You lost or sumtin'?" He laughed as he scratched his leg with the barrel of the gun. Strange Willie pressed his nose against the screen. Hampton did the same, looking up at this strange character with mournful, hungry eyes. Strange Willie hitched his pants and angrily kicked the bottom of the door. The mesh crushed against Hampton's face making him stand up. Hampton wasn't experienced enough to take this as a warning of what was

about to come. Instead, he barked again, wagging his tail in a friendly fashion. Hampton loved people.

"You hungry, dawg?" Strange Willie asked. "You wanna dance for yor suppa?"

Strange Willie stepped back from the door, went to the counter, and quickly returned with a slab of pork ribs, mostly fat. He held up the meat, teasing Hampton whose tongue licked his lips.

" Want sum pork, boy?"

Standing on his hind legs, Hampton put his front feet on the screen door to get as close as he could to the tempting meal. Strange Willie pushed open the door, sending Hampton tumbling backwards onto the flat stones that formed the doorstep. He squealed in pain as he landed on his sore leg.

Strange Willie laughed as he threw the meat onto the dirt road in front of the trailer home. Despite the pain, Hampton chased the meat onto the road. As Hampton ran, Strange Willie raised the gun to his shoulder, brought the hound into the sights and squeezed the trigger. Luckily for Hampton Strange Willie couldn't focus clearly this early in the morning and the buckshot sailed harmlessly over the hound's head. The loud blast from the shotgun sent Hampton scurrying into a nearby stand of trees where he hid behind a large beech tree. Many times before he had heard the crack of the Master's whip, which was nothing compared to the loud bang from Strange Willie's shotgun. Although the blast had scared him, he hadn't felt any pain. He didn't know that the deadly pellets had flown inches over his head. As far as Hampton knew, the long metal pole Strange Willie held in his hand made a lot of noise, but it wouldn't hurt him.

"C'mon, dawgie. Here dawg...c'mon and eat," Strange Willie called to Hampton. White smoke trickled from the end of the gun.

Hampton peered cautiously from behind the tree. And with his tail between his legs he slowly crept back toward the meat that Strange Willie used as bait. As Hampton crawled out of the woods, Strange Willie lifted the gun back up to his shoulder. This time he took better aim. A bead of sweat trickled down his brow as Strange Willie tried focusing on the hound. The image went in and out of focus behind the small bead that was used to aim the gun. Strange Willie blinked twice to steady the image. Now the hound was clear in his sights. A second droplet of sweat pinged the ground as Strange Willie's muscles tightened and he began squeezing the trigger.

At that instant a small animal darted across the field just beyond where Hampton was crossing the road and where Strange Willie was aiming the gun. It was a blurry flash that Strange Willie saw out of the corner of his eye. In the split second before he could squeeze the trigger, Strange Willie's attention was diverted and, as the gun went off, he swung the barrel away from the unwary hound. Lucky for Hampton the shot missed its mark. However, one of the pellets grazed Hampton's skin just above his left shoulder and to his surprise it hurt. It was a lesson learned just in time. The gun not only made a lot of noise, the pellets that came out of it with a loud bang and a puff of smoke could hurt him. That was enough to send Hampton racing back into the cover of the sheltering beech trees. Strange Willie was not happy. He looked around and fired another blast into the brush by the side of the road where he had seen the red, furry animal dart under the low branches of a dogwood thicket. He squeezed the trigger again, but both barrels of the gun were empty and the extra ammunition lay on the floor of the trailer next to his bedroll a safe distance away.

"He'll be back," muttered Strange Willie to no one in particular, because he was alone in the yard. He scratched his dirty head with his left hand, pivoted on his boot heel, and stomped back inside the trailer. “Then I’ll get him. No uppity dawg’s gonna fool with Strange Willie.”

From his cover under the beeches, Hampton watched Strange Willie go back into the trailer. The screen door slammed shut behind the raggedy man and Hampton’s attention drifted back to the meat lying a short distance away, tantalizing his taste buds. Hampton stared at his would-be breakfast wondering how to get it without drawing the attention of that oddball person with the smoking gun. Then the strangest thing happened.

With the swiftness of a swooping hawk, a red fox, the same one who had distracted Strange Willie and had made

him miss killing Hampton, darted out of the woods. With lightning speed he grabbed the meat in his jaws and raced back to the safety of the thicket. It took place so quickly Hampton barely knew what happened. Strange Willie obviously didn't notice the commotion, because he stayed hidden within his hovel.

The sun was bringing late autumn warmth to the valley but that didn't help fill Hampton's empty stomach. The lost hound was still very hungry.

Hampton wondered what to do next.

CHAPTER 8

Carly looked up from her math homework as the blast from the shotgun echoed through the hills. Gunshots were common and Carly didn't think too much about the sound. Somebody was always shooting somewhere in the thousand-acre woods surrounding the farm. It was part of life in the country. When the hunters weren't stalking birds or deer, they were shooting at tin cans or road signs. Carly wished people wouldn't kill the animals.

They were her friends. All of them. Her grandfather often cautioned her to keep clear of the hunters and to wear bright clothing in the woods. He didn't want the hunters mistaking Carly or her pony for a large deer. More than once a hunter's mistake had cost someone's life. It made Carly shudder to think about it, but she was only eleven-years-old and there wasn't much she could do to change the ways of guns and hunters. Her grandfather had a gun and once in a while he would take it out and shoot at some old bottles back where he burned the trash. He never used it for hunting. Occasionally, he would shoot at a critter like a woodchuck or raccoon after they messed up his vegetable garden. But he never hit anything. He often talked about shooting the pesky red fox that came visiting, but the fox always managed to stay out of harm's way.

Carly added the last column of math numbers, closed her book, and put it back in her canvas backpack. Her chores done, homework finished for the weekend, and the sun was out. It was time for a ride in the woods.

"Going out," Carly called to her grandfather who was in the backyard chopping wood for the coming winter. It seemed he always had something to do. Farm work, unlike homework, never ended.

"Where ya headed?" the old man inquired.

"I'm going to take Monroe out into the woods and look for the missing hound," she answered with a slight smile. She felt confident she would find the lost hound and become the heroine of Nottoway County. That's what she told herself the night before, as she fell asleep dreaming about finding the missing puppy. Maybe Mr. Drury would ask her to ride with the Hunt. Even up front with the staff.

"Have a good time and be careful," grandfather reminded her. He always told her the same thing. But this morning he had an extra warning. "I heard some shots a while back.

Seemed to be coming from Strange Willie's place. Don't know what he'd be firing at this early in the day. Raccoon perhaps. He's a strange bird. So be careful, be alert, and stay clear. Okay, Carly?"

"Sure, Grandpa. That place gives me the creeps, anyway," she said, giving her grandfather an affectionate kiss on the cheek. She skipped off to the barn where Monroe was finishing the last of his breakfast hay. He had rolled the day before in a large mud puddle and was caked, head to hoof, in red Virginia clay. It took Carly quite a while to get him clean again. While hard work, currying Monroe was part of the fun of owning a pony and one chore Carly didn't mind. She pretended she was getting ready for a big horse show, or even better, for the day she would ride with the Riverdale Hunt Club.

Monroe nickered a greeting as Carly entered his stall armed with a currycomb and brush. An hour later she would be in the saddle heading down the winding road that led away from the farm into the woods. It was a beautiful day.

CHAPTER 9

Hampton couldn't believe the brashness of the red fox that had stolen his breakfast. Not only was that horrible man shooting at him, but now another creature had run away with his food. Hampton crept carefully through the shadow of the woods, as he started out after the red fox and the food. He watched the fox disappear into the tall grass but waited to make sure it was safe before setting out after him. He put his keen nose to the ground and circled the thicket where he thought the fox had been hiding. It wasn't long before he picked up the familiar scent, the smell he had been taught to follow since a puppy. His foot was feeling better.

The fox knew the woods well and expected Hampton would soon be on his trail. He had watched Strange Willie tantalizing the hound and knew the dog was no match for the military veteran. Over the years the fox had studied Strange Willie from the cover of the brush and several times himself had been the target of Strange Willie's wrath. He also knew that Strange Willie rarely hit anything he shot at and more than once the fox taunted him with his wily ways. While Hampton might not be a match for Strange Willie, the fox knew he could outwit him easily. It had become a game. Now there was a new player.

The fox knew Hampton was a young, inexperienced hound with little knowledge of the real world. He often sat on the hill above the kennels watching the hounds play. In their fenced yard they were protected from the pitfalls of the outside world. With Hampton lost in these woods, the fox knew it was up to him to protect the hound until the humans came for him.

So he grabbed the pork and ran off with it, luring Hampton away from danger. Every so often as he ran, the fox leaped onto a rock or tree stump making sure the hound followed his scent. The fox stayed in view just long enough for

Hampton to get a quick glimpse of the meat he carried locked between his jaws.

The chase continued for the better part of an hour, past farmyards, through dense thickets and thorny bushes that clawed at Hampton's skin.

Then the trail led up over a hill and into a forest with a thick canopy. The sun cut beams through the trees where the branches were split enough to let a narrow ray of light through. The light splashed in reflecting pools at the roots of the trees, casting patterns of light and dark in which the two animals darted. At a place called The Rapids, they came to a fast running creek swollen by yesterday's heavy rain. Just above a spot where the water threw itself against the rocks creating whirlpools, quick falls, and whitewater rapids, a fallen tree less than a foot in diameter formed a natural bridge. The fox quickly took the challenge and like a tightrope walker danced across the narrow bridge, his body moving with the beat of the rushing water ten feet below. He had practiced this crossing hundreds of times since the tree blew over in a gale last January. The fox glanced over his shoulder and there, right on cue, was Hampton at the foot of the fallen tree.

Hampton was not sure about the crossing. He never had to negotiate a fallen tree spanning a flooded creek. Each jagged rock below dared Hampton to take the first step, to accept the challenge. One false step, Hampton knew, would surely mean a fall into the rapids, something Hampton wanted to avoid at all costs. Slowly he moved out across the rippled bark of the fallen red swamp maple. Dying autumn leaves, now turned burgundy red, still hung on the outstretched branches that seemed to be reaching out to break the fall, as the tree bowed to the wind. Hampton had all four legs on the tree trunk. He took one step forward. Then a second, third, and fourth. Suddenly, he felt himself losing his balance. He leaned hard to the right, then left, then back to the right. It was no use. Hampton lost his balance and tumbled off the tree, crashing onto a soft patch of mossy grass.

Luckily, he was still over solid ground when he completely lost his balance and fell. Unhurt, Hampton jumped right back up onto the tree. He had made a slight mistake the first time around but wouldn't fall again. Tree walking was under control. The red fox watched from a perch safely on the far side of the stream. In his heart, he was rooting for Hampton to make it across.

Hampton was ready to try again. Now he was out on the tree trunk.

Now he was moving slowly. Now he was going more quickly. Now he was dancing across the tree-bridge like he had witnessed the agile fox moments earlier. Hampton was proud of himself and he arched his back to show the world how good he was at walking on trees. He tilted his head vainly toward the sky not noticing that the tree was getting smaller in diameter as he reached what had been the topmost branches. Posturing like he was, he couldn't see the jagged broken branch directly in his footpath.

Hampton stepped on the sharp edge with his hurt foot, which sent bolts of pain through his leg causing Hampton to once again lose balance. His feet scrambled frantically and with outstretched toenails tried grasping the slippery bark. But he couldn't find the grip. The turbulent water howled below. Hampton fell to his left; certain he was bound for the rapids. But the same broken branch that caused his fall straddled two larger branches just below the tree trunk forming a safety net into which Hampton fell. Only his pride was hurt. Hampton lay still for a minute catching his breath. He was panting very heavily and his heart raced. The fox sat up on his hind legs for a better view of the action.

Hampton realized he was only six feet from the other side. Somehow, he must climb back onto the tree and carefully walk the remaining two yards to safety. This time he would not take his eyes off the tree trunk until his feet touched the solid earth on the opposite creek bank. Hampton reached out for the main trunk with his front legs. He had to lock them around the tree trunk and then swing his back legs over and onto its surface. A good trick for a circus dog, much less a foxhound. Hampton looked at the rushing water below. Much to his surprise, he saw another branch, slim but sturdy, some six inches below where he crouched. This made the trick a little more reasonable. Cautiously, he reached down with one back leg, a second leg, then slowly slid his body down the leaves, until all four legs were resting on the branch which led directly back to the main trunk. Hampton inched his way along. It took him almost ten minutes to walk the last few feet, each step planned and deliberate, insuring his success. Once back on firm ground, Hampton sat down in a nearby shallow pool of water for a drink and a well-deserved rest. The fox would just have to wait.

CHAPTER 10

Carly's pony, Monroe, sparkled in the morning light after his bath and grooming. As she did with her pony, Carly kept the saddle and bridle clean and polished. Monroe danced in place as she made sure her girth was tight and the stirrup leathers just the right length. He was eager to get underway, to take his partner on today's adventure, wherever that might lead. Carly vaulted into the saddle with the grace of an Olympic gymnast. She rode an English jumping saddle with an Italian name. She turned Monroe's head with light pressure on the right rein and urged him forward with pressure from her legs. He responded immediately and they headed west down the dirt road leading into her grandfather's cornfields, where yellowed stalks stood as a silent tribute to the recent harvest. The road, pitted with deep ruts her grandfather's

tractor made during last spring's mud season, wound and turned. Water stood in the deeper depressions where a warm mist rose in the cool morning air. Monroe didn't like getting his feet wet, so he carefully weaved in and around any wet spots. While the puddles were to be avoided, Monroe trotted straight through the numerous streams and brooks that criss-crossed the land.

At a corner where the cornfield met a pasture, Carly confronted a large, hinged gate. Monroe knew the routine well and he slowly edged up to the latched end, so Carly could open it without dismounting. The gate swung easily and Carly and the pony hurried through before the gate swung shut. Before continuing on, she leaned over and latched the metal gate, keeping the farm animals safely fenced inside.

Through the pasture, the worn trail crossed gently rolling hills. Carly signaled Monroe with her legs and the pony quickly stepped out in an evenly paced trot. The young rider rose in and out of the saddle, posting to the beat of Monroe's cadence. A few hundred yards away, a small herd of black Angus cows grazed peacefully. Two young steer played aggressively under the watchful eyes of their mothers. In recent years, her grandfather's stock had dwindled to several dozen. During better economic times, several hundred cows grazed these hillsides.

The grassy path led to a stone wall and a second gate which Carly handled easily. They passed quickly through the opening and headed off into the woods, which bordered the 200-acre farm. In a few moments she left her grandfather's property and entered a mature forest of native beech and hickory trees. With the trail providing a smooth cushion, Monroe picked up a collected canter rocking Carly gently in the saddle. She was one with the pony as they glided across the countryside, the gentle breeze causing her auburn hair to fan out below her helmet. Her pony's ears focused forward, as they approached a fallen tree across the path. Just yesterday, grandfather lectured her about jumping while riding alone in the woods. But Carly figured he meant the large stone walls or wooden jumps known as chicken coops which the Hunt used for their sport. A tiny tree on the trail didn't count, she thought, as Monroe sailed over the one-foot obstacle. In her mind, Carly could hear the horn of the hunt master and the piercing cries of the howling hounds, as she followed an imaginary hunt. Reins taut in her hands, the wind caressing her face, Carly cantered through the woods. Her mission to find the missing hound remained in the front of her thoughts. She glanced left and right looking for any trace, any glimpse of the hound or clues he may have left behind.

Carly slowed the pony to a trot, then a walk, as she approached a narrow stream swollen from the recent rains. Monroe sniffed the cascading water, then splashed through to dry ground. On the other side, the trail led downhill into a once-cultivated valley where the autumn brown grasses awaited the white snows of winter. A red-tail hawk made lazy circles in the sky, two hundred yards away on the southern horizon. Carly watched curiously as the soaring bird glided against a backdrop of puffy clouds.

Perhaps the hawk was stalking a stricken animal, waiting for it to die. The hawk rode the air currents effortlessly, as

Carly decided to investigate the area directly below where it hovered. She turned her pony in that direction and trotted off down a dirt road, fearful of what she might find.

Carly passed an abandoned shack, which at one time housed an irrigation water pump. One hundred yards further, she saw a pile of rocks and old boards. She was still a distance from the pile when the hawk dove from the sky and disappeared behind the heap. It emerged a short time later and returned to its observation point above the treetops. Uneasy, Carly urged her pony forward. What she really wanted to do was turn around and gallop off in the opposite direction but curiosity stopped her from turning back.

Her eyes half closed, Carly rode over a bridge of railroad ties until she could see the far side of the pile. Much to her relief, all she found was the carcass of a deer that died of old age. She looked toward the sky where the hawk was making tighter and tighter circles. The hawk looked back at her, the bird's menacing stare piercing deep into her own eyes. He looked angry and Carly couldn't blame him because she had interrupted his meal. Monroe, sharing her view of the hawk, shuffled his front legs nervously. He too thought they had overstayed their welcome and was eager to head down the trail. Carly turned her eyes from the hawk and asked Monroe to move out. It took very little urging on Carly's part to steer the pony back onto the path. She crouched forward in a jockey stance and Monroe broke into a full gallop. They rode for several minutes until they were a safe distance from the hawk. Sitting firmly in the saddle, she gave a slight tug with the reins, and Monroe responded instantly by slowing down to a trot, then a fast walk. Carly took a deep breath and looked back over her right shoulder where the hawk continued its waltz with the wind. It never bothered to look back at her as she left the area, but Carly knew that in the woods animals were always keenly aware of their surroundings. Carly rode away smiling. She loved this kind of adventure and was feeling increasingly more comfortable in the woods.

Often when Carly rode in the woods alone, thoughts of her parents drifted back to her. She had lived with Grandpa Oakley for two years while her parents served in the military overseas. Either her mom or dad would visit every six months or so, but usually they couldn't get the same vacation leave. It had been almost eighteen months since she had seen both parents together. Her dad's tour of duty with the Marines was scheduled to end just after Christmas and he'd be coming home to the farm. Her mom had six months more to serve in the Navy where she flew jet fighters. Carly loved her mom and was very proud that she was the only kid she knew, either here or back home in Dayton, Ohio, with a mom who flew jet airplanes. When Carly was little her mom took her for a ride in one of the fastest planes the Navy flies. It was a thrill she never forgot, but she loved riding her pony more. Carly missed her mom and nightly she marked off on her calendar the number of days until her return.

She often lay in bed late at night wondering about the future. Her dad wrote telling Carly that when he returned in January they would be staying at the farm, at least until they were permanently reunited with her mom. Then they would decide as a family where the rest of their journey through life would take them. Carly already knew how she would vote. She wanted to stay in the country, on a farm like her grandfather's.

She gave Monroe a little pat on his neck, reassuring him that she wasn't going to leave him. They protected each other, walking through the meadow, neither one knowing where the next turn might lead.

CHAPTER 11

Strange Willie was grumpier than ever as he awoke from his short after-breakfast nap. That incident with the hound made him very sleepy and, as he slipped off into his dream world, he grumbled to himself about missing that "dang dawg" from twenty yards away. Now he was awake, upset because he had on only one sock – a dirty rag that hadn't seen soap or water in more than a month. He couldn't remember when he had taken off the other sock or even where he left it. Uttering a few groans, he pulled on his old logging boots, the left one going onto a sockless foot. He wore farmer's overalls, although the only farming he did was in a little garden behind his trailer. Once every so often he would pull a tomato or cucumber from the tangled vines that grew amid the dirt, rocks, and weeds. Strange Willie didn't remember to water the garden, so its growth was sporadic at best, which didn't matter much, because he was just as likely to forget to eat lunch or dinner. His main meal was breakfast, consisting of toast and eggs from the old hen that lived in a small pen behind the trailer. On special occasions like Thanksgiving a few strips of bacon would adorn his plate. He had stopped giving thanks early in life, shortly after he returned from the war in Vietnam, forty years ago.

Strange Willie was thin and pale, his face drawn and haggard. He peered out into the world through tired, bloodshot eyes. The overalls he wore were three sizes too big and very baggy. The left strap hook fell off several years ago and now the bib hung half open across the front of his chest, revealing a torn black tee shirt with a Guns & Roses logo on the front. From a distance, he looked like one of those wild-haired, hip-hop city kids he had seen on his nine-inch portable, black and white television set. Tin foil wrapped around the rabbit-ear antennae helped bring in a blurry picture on this relic from the early days of television. It had been the only link Strange Willie had to the real world, except every other month or so when he rode his Harley chopper into town eight miles away for supplies and to pick up his monthly disability check delivered to a post office box. Now even the TV didn't work anymore. Something about not being digital. Something he didn't fully understand.

Strange Willie shuffled over to his unmade bed where he placed his shotgun before his nap. He picked up the weapon by its barrel and slung it over his shoulder, marching like a bad soldier into the yard. An old Campbell's chicken soup can lay discarded in the path. Strange Willie kicked it once, putting a dent in the side. Then he picked it up, walked twenty yards across the path and placed the rusty can on a tree stump, two feet off the ground. The stump was one of Strange Willie's most valuable assets. He used the table-like structure for dozens of purposes like chopping wood or skinning wild animals. Sometimes it became a chair or a table, but today it was a pedestal for his target practice. The can leaned left like the Tower of Pisa, so Strange Willie tilted his head in the same direction. He lifted the gun to his shoulder, aimed carefully, then stopped before his finger pulled the trigger. The can had fallen over. Strange Willie kicked a mushroom off its stem, walked over and set the can straight again with the help of a small, oval-shaped stone. He paced back to his firing position and brought the shotgun back to his shoulder. He pulled the trigger of the gun sending the spray of pellets ten feet over the can and stump. A hen flapped its startled wings. A black snake awoke from its sleep in the sun and scurried back into

the cover of the forest. Strange Willie squeezed off a second shot which missed the target seven feet to the left. He wasn't even coming close to hitting the can. His face turned red as he reached into his pocket searching for a second round of ammunition. His greasy hand came back empty and he snorted as he stomped back to the trailer where he had left his box of shells. Running out of them seemed to be a pattern of behavior, one that had saved Hampton's life hours earlier.

CHAPTER 12

The woods were dark and dense and the sun had to fight for a small space in which to wedge a beam. Carly was where she should not have been.

Her grandfather told her over a hundred times to stay away from Baker's Swamp, home to bobcat, bear, snakes, and Strange Willie. Along the edge of a muddy creek she followed what appeared to be very distinct dog tracks that led along a winding path through the thick forest. She had never ventured out this far by herself, although with her grandfather they passed this way several times. The woods seemed scarier now that she was by herself. Monroe would warn her of danger and no one would have to tell Grandpa she had disobeyed him. If she went south and skirted the woods around Strange Willie's she might never pick up the hound's tracks on the other side. And if anything were to happen, she'd give Monroe his head and he'd race her away as he had done earlier at the hawk incident.

Carly didn't totally understand why Strange Willie was so hated.

Beyond the dirty clothes, behind the ratty beard, was just another human.

There were widespread rumors about his anti-social

behavior and some of her classmates told her that he skinned kids alive. She knew that wild animals would attack when threatened and perhaps Strange Willie acted the way he did because he felt cornered by encroaching civilization. Her dad told stories about that terrible war many years before she was born and Grandpa Oakley once mentioned that when Strange Willie came back from that distant land, he acted funny and strange. That's why people started calling him Strange Willie. He'd been in mental hospitals twice and once in prison but only because someone said they thought they saw him break into a store at night. It turned out Strange Willie wasn't anywhere near town when the burglary happened and several weeks later another man confessed to the crime. After that, Strange Willie sank deeper into a shell, shooting at trespassers who wandered onto his small parcel of land. Carly had seen Strange Willie in town on a couple of occasions and had tried to make herself look invisible as he passed her on the sidewalk. Once, while her grandfather shopped at Ben's Corner Variety, she sat on the fender of their Dodge and watched Strange Willie from a distance. He seemed to be caught in a time warp between two "No Parking" signs, walking back and forth babbling to himself.

Images of Strange Willie flashed through Carly's mind as Monroe trotted over a rise in the trail where roots poked through the loose earth.

She saw the leaves in the trees rustle an instant before she heard the blast from the shotgun. The pellets flew safely over her head, but the blast startled Monroe as much as it did Carly. He stopped short, whirling around on his hind end.

Unfortunately, Carly reacted in the opposite direction, lost her balance, and was thrown over the pony's shoulder onto a bed of pine needles. The fall knocked the wind out of her but otherwise she was uninjured. Monroe sensed the danger and trotted a few yards down the path away from the gunshot. Gasping for air, Carly called out a faint, "Monroe, no." Monroe stopped in his tracks, twisted his head, and watched Carly as she slowly rose to her feet.

"What a good pal," Carly spoke aloud, as Monroe waited for her to catch up. Not quite able to run, her pace was quicker than a walk as she returned to her pony's side. With a sigh she swung herself up into the saddle and at a gallop retraced

her route up the path, hugging Monroe's back as he raced away from the exposed danger. Both the girl and pony breathed heavily as Carly listened for another shot, but the woods were silent, except for the surge of air from her pony's nostrils, the beat of his hooves along the path, and the rush of the wind past Carly's ears. When she was a mile down the road, Carly reined the pony in and he slowed to a trot. She felt she was safe but just in case wanted to put more space between herself and that crazy man. She continued trotting for another ten minutes before finally feeling totally out of danger. Carly breathed a heavy sigh of relief. Monroe did likewise.

CHAPTER 13

Hampton enjoyed the cool dampness of the shallow pool in which he rested. Knowing he had stayed too long, he stretched as he rose to his feet sniffing alternately the air and the ground. The sun was high in the sky and the day had turned unusually warm for October, the temperature nearing 80 degrees. A short distance away, his bushy tail wrapped around his body, the red fox sat in the tall grasses waiting for Hampton's return to the chase. Little did Hampton know that the fox was leading him away from danger. If only the hound would pick up the cue and follow him toward safety. The fox purposely left a strong scent near where Hampton stopped to catch his breath and now his keen sense of smell picked up that scent. From his perch, the fox could see the tip of Hampton's tail as it started toward where he was sitting. It was time to leave as the fox leaped forward, his strong back legs propelling him down the trail. Visions of breakfast were strong in Hampton's mind as he followed the fox into the hardwood forest, where hemlock and poplar, basswood, beech, white ash, and oak trees stood proud and tall. The trail was getting steeper as it meandered through the forest and Hampton panted harder as he climbed to a higher elevation.

The path led to a log cabin, long ago abandoned by a mountain family who could no longer eek out a meager existence, as civilization continued to lean on the simpler life of bygone days. In another time there would have been smoke drifting up from a hearth fire where iron pots would have been filled with the awaiting dinner. A half-cord of split oak logs was piled on the front porch where they had been left to rot. Once there would have been children laughing as they ran barefoot through the yard, taunting an old dog who lay sleeping lazily on the front stoop. Now the home stood empty.

Hand-hewn logs, once tightly notched together, were no longer a match for the wind, as it whistled through the walls on stormy days. Large, gaping holes were numerous in the shingled roof and did little to keep out the rain or snow.

Without hesitation, the red fox ran up onto the front porch, pausing momentarily to make sure Hampton was close at hand. Then he darted through the rotting wooden door, which hung precariously on one hinge.

Before entering the cabin, the fox did another strange thing. Strange in the world of wild animals. He dropped the

piece of pork that he carried for several miles since leaving Strange Willie's. Dropped it deliberately, before he disappeared into the shadows of the log cabin where shafts of sunlight broke through the roof panels. Hampton watched in disbelief. He stopped twenty yards from the front stoop, hesitant to move forward, fearing another deadly trap like the one he had experienced earlier in Strange Willie's yard. A small, cottontail rabbit watched from the safety of the broom sedge, whose tall brown stalks provided a perfect hiding place. Hampton inched forward toward the food, his body slinking low to the ground, his ears at attention listening for any sound of alarm, his nose leading the way. His head bobbed left and right as he crawled closer and closer to the slab of pork. A morning dove broke cover and fluttered noisily into the cloudless sky, as a silent jet passed high overhead. Hampton froze in his tracks, making himself as small as possible.

The bird flew away leaving silence in its wake. Hampton didn't move for several minutes. Nothing stirred, no other noises. As the fox watched from a roost in a window opening, Hampton slowly gathered his courage. The muscles tightened in his haunches, and, like a coiled rattlesnake striking without warning, the hound leaped through the air landing on top of the meat. With a quick snap of his jaws, the awaiting food was in his mouth. Hampton bolted back into the tall grass, sending the rabbit bounding off in the opposite direction. Two gulps later, the slab of pork was history and Hampton licked his lips as he sat panting heavily in the grass. In the distance the roar of a Harley motorcycle rippled through the hillside, but it was so far away that Hampton, savoring the moment, did not notice.

CHAPTER 14

Carly could hear the rumble of the motorcycle in the distance but paid little attention. Over the hill was the highway, she thought, where lots of cars, trucks, and motorcycles sped by to wherever it was they were going. It never ceased to amaze Carly that, whenever she went riding in an automobile, there were always hundreds of other vehicles on the highway. She wondered where these people were going all the time and why they were always in such a hurry.

Monroe pricked his ears forward and slowed his gait. He was on alert.

He sensed danger in the air. At first Carly thought her pony was responding to the sound of the rapidly approaching motorcycle. Monroe suddenly shied, kicking out. Carly heard a hissing sound and then a thud, as the pony's left hind hoof came squarely in contact with the onrushing animal, sending it careening backwards. She saw the black and white ball of fur land on its back and disappear into thick underbrush, only its bushy tail remaining in sight. Carly had seen many skunks before, but this was puzzling. She knew they only ventured out at night. Unless, of course, they are sick.

A chill ran through Carly's body. Dizzy, unsteady. Her balance on Monroe's back wavered. She remembered recent newspaper accounts of rabies running rampant and knew the deadly disease could turn an infected animal's behavior upside down. Not only did they act strangely, they became aggressive monsters, attacking anything and everything in their path. Carly felt the woods closing in on her. Monroe pawed the earth, his nostril flared red with each breath. Carly knew she must get away as quickly as she could, but she was frozen in place. While her brain kept telling her what to do, her muscles did not respond. She wondered if Monroe had killed the skunk with his kick. She was thankful that her pony had all of his vaccinations, including one for rabies. Several horses on a farm in the next county had taken ill with rabies and had to be put down. They hadn't even been bitten.

Carly learned on the radio that a sick raccoon had broken into a grain storage barrel and had left rabies-infested saliva on the horses' feed. Monroe's food was kept sealed in a large feed bin with a strong latch-bolt.

Just as Carly was regaining her senses, the stricken skunk sprang from the bushes, glaring at Carly through glazed, fiery-red eyes. Its black tail, with the highway of white running through it, flicked angrily from side to side. Behind a beard of foamy, gray saliva, razor sharp teeth showed pearly white. For the second time in less than a minute, Carly froze in the saddle, not even able to scream. The wild animal charged, covering ten yards in a fraction of a second. Mustering all of its strength, the skunk sprung off its back legs and hurled itself toward the frightened girl. While running, the skunk seemed to be fast as a lighting bolt, but once in the air, it seemed to float toward Carly in slow motion. Was it real or was she in the middle of a horrible nightmare?

The blast from the shotgun sent shock waves through the hillside, the noise so loud that Carly thought it was right next to her ear. Monroe startled again and reared, dumping Carly backward onto the hard, scratchy ground.

The entire scene blurred out of focus as she lay on the ground. When her vision cleared a moment later, she saw two things that made her feel safe, yet extremely frightened, at the same time. On the ground, not ten feet away lay the dead body of the sick skunk, the air thick with its familiar rank odor.

What really shocked Carly was the silhouette of a ragged man sitting on a large motorcycle a short distance away, half-hidden by the sprawling limbs of an evergreen. Resting across the handlebars was a long-barreled shotgun, a trickle of smoke filtering toward the sky. A lone tear wandered down Carly's cheek followed by a flood of uncontrollable crying. Tears of relief, fear, happiness, and pain merged, washing away the stinging, oily perfume that the skunk shot into the air.

Monroe ate grass two hundred yards away, the reins wrapped precariously around his right leg. The man on the motorcycle sat silently.

Carly's tears stopped flowing, but her eyes remained red and puffy. Wiping her nose on her sleeve, she slowly rose to her knees where she could see more clearly and immediately recognized the man on the motorcycle. The name, "Strange Willie," formed on her lips, but no sounds came out. She was embarrassed but wanted to thank him for saving her life. While his presence was ominous and foreboding, there was a gentleness about Strange Willie which Carly never noticed before in her brief encounters with him, but now she saw plainly in his eyes. She wanted to reach out, hold his hand and give him a huge hug, but her legs were still shaky and she wasn't yet able to stand. So they sat there in silence, each not speaking. Finally, Carly found the strength to stand and the courage to speak.

"Thanks, mister. Thanks for..." she stammered.

Strange Willie cut her off. "No need ta thank me. That pony a yers sent a message...said you was in trouble."

Seeing that Carly was not injured, Strange Willie revved his Harley, spun the wheels, and roared down the trail, leaving the young girl speechless. Monroe whinnied to her and Carly realized the pony needed her attention. She untangled the reins, remounted, and soon they were racing the sun toward home. As she rode, Carly wondered what Strange Willie had meant. How could Monroe have sent him a danger signal, an animal S.O.S?

CHAPTER 15

The sun was hanging low in the October sky, casting long shadows across the yard. Grandpa Oakley tugged at his thermal vest. Late afternoons turned cool quickly, especially with a Northeast wind blowing. The farmer checked his watch and looked up, shielding his eyes from the sun's glare.

Coming out of the shadows, he saw Monroe and his granddaughter trotting down the path toward home.

"Just about time," he shouted as the pony drew closer. "Another few minutes and I'd have started to worry about you two."

"Now Grandpa," Carly retorted. "You knew I'd be home before dark. Always am. You can count on me."

"Sure can, like you have a built-in clock in your brain," her grandfather said. "It's Monroe can't tell time." Then he let out a big laugh.

Carly joined in the laughter and Monroe shook his head. The pony pranced in place, knowing that hay and oats awaited him in his stall.

Dinner was never late at the Oakley farm. As Carly approached her grandfather, the lingering odor from the encounter with the skunk pervaded the air. Her grandfather sniffed then exhaled, "Phwew, got a little too close to Mother Nature, eh Carly?"

"We didn't see the skunk until it was too late," she confessed, leaving out many details of the episode with the skunk and Strange Willie. She knew her grandfather would be very upset if he knew she disobeyed him.

"Get the pony cleaned up, and yourself, too. Then we'll think about supper. Your turn to cook."

Without breaking stride, Carly jumped from the saddle and continued trotting alongside Monroe toward the barn. She unbuckled the girth, traded the bridle for a halter, and gave Monroe a quick grooming. His emerging winter coat showed the stress of the ride and was matted with mud where the saddle and girth had been. The curry comb felt good on his skin, but he wanted to eat more than he wanted to look pretty, and the skunk smell was just part of living with nature. Carly scolded him for prancing in place.

Darkness prowled across the valley and most creatures were preparing for nightfall by the time Carly finished cleaning the pony. She bolted the door to Monroe's stall and said goodnight, giving him a kiss on the forehead. A common barn owl flew from its perch in a tall fir tree, following a small mouse as it scurried for home. A coyote bayed in the distance. A mother raccoon put her brood safely in their pine tree nest, before heading out to prowl for food in unguarded garbage cans.

Down the road in his trailer, Strange Willie kicked off his boots and stoked the fire in the wood stove. A freshly killed pheasant lay ready for frying next to the rusty kitchen sink. He was pleased at having saved the young girl and her pony from the rabid skunk. When a life was in jeopardy, his military training took over and he responded deftly, without self-doubt. He was also pleased that no one had seen him do it. He didn't need any attention from anyone in these parts. Just knowing in his own mind that he had done a good deed was reward enough. During the war many years ago, a friend saved his life in some unnamed rice paddy. Moments later the friend, he still remembered his name, Alfred Cousins, was killed by shrapnel from an exploding bomb. The tragedy was that the bomb was from so-called friendly fire, dropped off-target by US aircraft. Alfred Cousins went home a hero in a wooden box. A hatful of ribbons for his children. Strange Willie didn't need to be a hero. He didn't care much what the folks thought about him, as long as they left him alone. The grease began to smoke in the skillet and his stomach gurgled. He was hungry.

At the old log cabin deep in the forest, a tired hound dug a hole next to a rotting stump and crawled in for the night. Somehow he felt safe, like someone or something was watching over him. Hampton couldn't see the two green eyes of the red fox watching him through the paneless window twenty yards away. It had been a long, eventful day and he was tired. He was no longer wet or hungry. Two good signs. In the morning he would continue his journey home. A lonely cloud drifted across the orange harvest moon as it peeked over the treetops. Hampton closed his eyes and quickly fell asleep. He was good at that.

Carly looked up from her stool in front of her sink where she was scrubbing the last of the dinner dishes. Tuna casserole, a fresh garden salad, and two brownies with vanilla ice cream had been her choice for dinner. The rule was that whoever prepared dinner could choose the menu.

Of course, it couldn't just be Oreo cookies and M & M's. Her grandfather made that very clear shortly after Carly moved in. Once in a while they ordered pizza out and Carly enjoyed the drive into town after dark to pick it up. She would sit buckled in the front seat of the Dodge pickup peering into the dark woods imagining the eyes of all kinds of strange animals staring back at her. The woods were dark and ominous and Carly would scare herself just thinking about being lost there. Her Grandpa always told her to stop putting those crazy thoughts into her brain, but Carly wouldn't listen.

Having grown up in the suburbs of a large city, the woods were a place she had to get to know slowly.

Now looking out into the darkness from the safety of her kitchen she thought she saw in the moonlight a small animal dart across the path. She blinked and the animal was gone. Her grandfather stood behind Carly looking over her shoulder.

"Did you see that, Grandpa?" Carly asked.

"Hope it wasn't that dang fox," he replied as he scrutinized the darkness. He flipped a switch on the wall, which fed electricity to a light on a pole over the entrance to the barn. The yard was bright, but empty.

Nothing moved.

"Might have been a rabbit," Carly offered, hoping her grandfather wouldn't get his shotgun and chase the fox. If it had been the fox. Carly hoped it wasn't. She rinsed the final glass tumbler, put it in the rack to dry, and jumped down from the small stool she used to reach the sink. She didn't really need the stool to wash the dishes, but it gave her a better view of the yard, so she liked using it.

"Rabbit can't do much harm this time of year. But a fox will rob you blind," her Grandpa said.

Carly didn't answer. Grandpa Oakley switched off the outdoor light, returning the barnyard to the critters of the night, and moved to the living room where he sank into his overstuffed chair. Carly came in and sat on her heels on the rug in front of her grandfather. Buster the cat seeing an opening snuggled into Carly's lap. After a short cleaning session, he yawned, closed his eyes, and fell asleep. The yawn was catching and passed from Buster to Carly to Grandpa Oakley.

"Another long day," her grandfather sighed.

"Can animals talk?" she blurted out.

"Sure," her grandfather said. "They talk to each other all the time."

"No, I mean to you and me? To people?" she wanted to know.

"Well, we talk to them, don't we?" he assured her.

"All the time," she answered.

"So I guess they talk to us. It's just that we don't always understand what they're saying, is all." He knew Carly wasn't asking a frivolous question and together they had read all about the experiments where people tried communicating with dolphins. And didn't that monkey woman, Jane what's-her-face, converse with the apes in Africa? These thoughts tumbled through his brain, but he didn't share them with his granddaughter.

"Do you think they can talk to us through thin air, you know, like with ESP?" The trashy newspapers she leafed through at Foodrite Grocery Store were filled with stories about psychics having conversations with dead people or relatives from another planet. She sometimes thought she could read her pony's mind. She gave up trying to communicate with Buster. He never had anything on his mind except eating.

"Don't know," Grandpa replied. "Guess I've had one or two things happen in my life I couldn't explain. And dang it all, if I don't hear from your Grandma, bless her soul, every time I get myself in a stupid jam." The only kind of trouble

Grandpa usually got into was forgetting where he parked his truck when he took Carly to the mall, an activity he dreaded but one that Carly insisted upon if she were to grow into any kind of normal teenager. Fortunately for the old man, the outings took place only a couple of times a year.

"Do you think they'll ever find the missing hound?" There was sadness in her voice as she asked the question, knowing her grandfather really didn't know the answer. But his voice was soothing, and, after this exhausting day, Carly needed to be reassured. While she wished she could tell her grandfather what really happened, she was too tired to face the consequences.

"I'm sure they will, Carly. Besides, that ole' hound dog can take care of itself. They're made of steel, you know." The image of a dog made of steel made her smile. Then she

thought of what would happen if a steel animal were caught out in the rain.

"You don't think it'll rust do you?" she asked suppressing a giggle.

Her grandfather tuned into the image of the rusting steel dog and let out one of his famous laughs. Buster opened one eye annoyed with the laughter, which caused Carly's knees to twitch, disturbing his rest. He didn't find any humor in dogs, steel or otherwise.

"Homework in place?" her grandfather asked.

"Yup," Carly said as she rested her head against the old man's knee.

She shut her eyes and reviewed the day's adventure. As the images played out in her brain, she felt herself drifting off to sleep. In her half-conscious state, her mind wandered back to when she was a very little girl, falling asleep in her father's arms. She missed her father and wished he were here with her. He'd be good at finding missing hounds. And maybe he knew if animals could send signals to people. Although puzzling, it was her last thought before sleep shut out the real world.

CHAPTER 16

The yellow school bus rumbled down the country road bouncing the children around at every bump. Inside there was muffled laughter as weekend adventures were shared with friends. Carly's best school friend, Freddie Wheeler, sat next to her on the bench seat chewing his thumb.

Freddie had a slim body with a large round head that from a distance made it look like a pumpkin sitting on a pole. He listened intently as Carly told her story. She spoke in soft tones barely audible above the din of the highway as the miles slipped along. When she finished, the two friends sat quietly, Carly looking into the woods and fields, Freddie into his lunch pail examining what his mom packed for lunch. They didn't speak for several moments. The bus stopped at a railroad crossing, then inched across the tracks before continuing on its way.

"I don't believe you," Freddie said breaking the silence. Carly didn't answer. Her gaze was fixed on a brown and white animal she saw trotting through a small stand of poplar trees less than five hundred yards away. She tried to focus closer on the image, wishing she could use her eyes like binoculars. The bus was going too fast and in a flash the animal was out of sight.

"Did you see that?" Carly asked her companion. Freddie's attention was riveted on the lunch box, an animated scene from a Disney cartoon. He looked up and out the window, but all he could see swishing past the window was a decaying farm stand next to an abandoned apple orchard.

"Nope," he said curtly. "I think you dreamed all of this. Maybe you're still dreaming." He went to pinch her on the cheek, but Carly was too fast and grabbed his wrist in a vise-like grip, giving him a quick wrist burn. The boy grimaced in pain and quickly apologized for teasing her.

“Want part of my Baby Ruth candy bar?” Freddie offered trying to appease his friend.

“No thanks,” she said loosening the tight grip around his wrist.

“Sorry, I didn’t mean to hurt you.”

Freddie rubbed his wrist, bright red from the burn. “That’s okay. Didn’t hurt a bit. I owe you one.”

The bus chugged down the highway leaving the incident behind. They sat in silence. Carly wondered if she had really seen the missing hound. Freddie wondered how long it would be until lunch. He had already eaten the candy bar and was again chewing on his finger. After school they would meet and continue the adventure.

CHAPTER 17

Hampton stretched. He felt good after a full night's sleep. Several times he was awakened by strange sounds coming from the dark woods.

This morning he was refreshed, but his muscles were sore from his long journey, and once again he was hungry. He wondered about the fox. He had seen the creature enter the shabby building the night before, after leaving Hampton a welcome dinner. Could miracles happen twice? Whether the fox was still inside or had slipped out during the night were beyond Hampton's comprehension. If the fox had slipped out, and Hampton knew they were slippery creatures from his brief exposure to their ways, he had managed to elude detection. Hampton was brash enough to think, for a minute, that perhaps the fox was out scrounging breakfast for them both. The idea was quickly replaced with the thought of having the fox for breakfast. Hampton wasn't to blame for this thought. It had been bred into his genes for hundreds of years. At the moment, there was no sign of the fox, and, besides, Hampton probably couldn't catch him anyway. His thoughts turned elsewhere. The hound knew he'd have to strike out on his own. Perhaps his only chance for a meal would come if he could find his way home. So off he went, tail standing tall, following his own scent, back along the trail on which he'd come. Hopefully, it would lead him out of the woods, out of trouble and back to his kennel and safety.

Unknown to Hampton, at that very moment several miles away, the fox was in a predicament of his own. He had ventured back to Strange Willie's trailer with the thought of retrieving some more scrap meat, an egg or two, or perhaps a stray chicken. He would share it with his new friend, the hound. But Strange Willie noticed the fox hanging around the last few weeks and was prepared to put a stop to his thievery. The day before he devised a makeshift trap out of an old fruit basket, a heavy rock, and a stick, using a freshly killed chicken as bait. It was a simple, yet effective, device that was sure to snare any greedy, uninvited creature that might come calling. He was right. Shortly before dawn, as the moon dove behind a distant mountain, along came the fox whose attention was immediately drawn to the awaiting bait. Jackpot. Two scores in less than twenty-four hours.

The fox crept slowly toward the trap, looked carefully left and right, and then pounced on the meat. As he turned to run away with the prize in his jaws, he bumped the stick holding up the edge of the basket. It gave way and the cage fell down, trapping the startled animal. Fortunately for the fox, his meal was still inside the basket with him. Hungry from his midnight prowls, the fox decided to take lunch while he figured a way out. After several large bites, which were quite filling, the fox came up with a solution. DIG. That's it. He would dig his way out.

The fox started digging frantically with his front paws. It

wasn't easy. The ground was a hard mixture of gravel and clay that had been packed down by the weight of a motorcycle rolling in an out of its parking space under a small canopy. The fox knew Strange Willie would wake soon and then he'd have no chance of escaping. The flying dirt smacked against the side of the basket as the fox dug, pinging as it hit. He could not see well enough through the basket slats to know that just about this time Hampton ambled down the trail, having followed his own scent all the way back to Strange Willie's small plot of land.

Out of the corner of his eye, Hampton saw a small cloud of dust spewing from beneath the old basket. A strange sight. At first he was wary, but, as his nose vacuumed the air, a familiar odor filled his nostrils. Fox. He was sure of it. Not only was it a fox, it was his friend the fox. Pay dirt. Miracles did happen twice. Hampton walked slowly to the edge of the trap and sniffed eagerly. The fox stopped digging and cringed in the basket, while Hampton walked slowly around its perimeter sniffing at the rim. The fox realized who it was and scratched a greeting with his paw against the slats. He hoped Hampton would recognize him. Hampton jumped on top of the circular trap looking for a way to get in, or get the fox out. Another dead end.

There seemed to be no way to get inside the overturned basket so the hound hopped off and circled the trap two more times, first in one direction, then the other. Standing on his hind legs, the hound placed his two front paws against the top edge of the basket and tried pushing. The basket, fox and all, slowly slid along the ground but it did not tip over. He tried this approach several more times with the same results. Finally, after pushing the basket in a complete circle back to where he had started, Hampton sat down to think. Most of all he thought about the food sitting just inches away.

Whether he actually thought of the scheme or just got up and acted out of frustration will always remain a mystery. Without hesitation, he madly charged the contraption. At full speed he slammed headfirst into the basket splintering the wood and tumbling with its contents in a ball of fury. On his feet first, the fox shot away to the safety of a large boulder. Hampton landed on his chin a yard away from what was left of the chicken. Normally he would have grabbed the meat and made a quick meal of it, but this wasn't a normal day. Something different was filling the air. Something black, acrid, with a smell that burned his nostrils. It came from the trailer.

Hampton's head turned quickly and followed the smoke back to where it originated, Strange Willie's trailer. He could see crimson flames licking out of a small vent on the roof and smoke billowing from every window, door, and crack. What made Hampton respond is not logical. He should have taken the meat and run as far and as fast as he could. Just the day before, Strange Willie had taken shots at him. Had tried to kill him. Then he trapped the fox.

But Hampton didn't run away. Instead he turned toward the trailer, and, with his head as low to the ground as possible, ran under the smoke toward the trailer door. The flames grew hotter as he approached the burning shelter. When he reached the door he found it open. Defying the danger, he charged inside, flames leaping over his head. There, still sleeping, was Strange Willie, his head hanging over the side of his makeshift bed. The night before, he hung his wet jeans on a thin clothesline over the woodstove to dry. Somehow, he failed to tie a sufficient knot and the clothesline drooped, leaving one leg inches from the open flame. It had taken several hours for the pants to dry, but once they did, they caught fire and like a torch set the rest of the trailer ablaze.

Hampton barked and licked the scruffy face of the hermit. Then he growled and softly bit his cheek. It was enough to awaken the man who slowly realized the danger he was in. He sat straight up in bed, grabbed his rifle and a spare pair of pants, and, like a panther, leaped toward the door, stumbling over Hampton. It was then he realized that this hound, which yesterday was the object of his wrath, had now returned to save his life. The two fugitives scrambled for the doorway, escaping seconds before the fire plunged from the ceiling and engulfed the entire trailer.

The fox watched from a safe distance, as the bonding between man and hound unfolded amidst the smoke and embers. Once outside, Strange Willie tried valiantly to douse the flames with a small bucket of water he refilled at the stream. It was little use other than keeping the flames from starting a massive forest fire. What he was really trying to do was keep the fire away from his prized motorcycle parked a few yards away. He could lose the trailer. There were other places he could live. Losing his Harley was not an option. Luckily, the recent heavy rains were on his side and the fire remained confined to the trailer that burned to the ground.

Hampton, meanwhile, sought refuge a safe distance away in a stream where he could watch the frantic activity. Once the fire cooled, he thought, he would retrieve the lost meal, then continue down the path toward home. Unfortunately for Hampton, Strange Willie spent the better part of the day sitting dazed on his motorcycle that stood directly between the hound and his chicken dinner. So Hampton dozed, off and on. It was a warm day and his stomach told him not to drift too far away from a certain meal. Anyway, there was no real hurry and Hampton had no clue where to go from here.

CHAPTER 18

Freddie and Carly met after school as promised. Today they rode mountain bikes because Freddie didn't have a pony like Monroe, had only once been on a horse, and didn't like it. Some people were born to be riders.
Others, like Freddie, shied away. This didn't keep them from being close friends, sharing secrets, and spending afternoons together exploring. Weekends, Freddie went to the city to live

with his dad, so Carly and Freddie would rendezvous after school on weekdays for their continuing adventures.

Throughout the day, Carly retold her fantastic story and, just after lunch, she knew Freddie finally believed her. Unpredictably, he suggested they continue the search for the missing hound, that he'd meet her at the Mill Street overpass at three o'clock. That would leave several hours before sunset, plenty of time for their exploration. Soon, daylight savings time would end, cutting their after school activity short during the winter months.

Freddie arrived at the meeting spot first and was busy studying animal prints in the mud, when Carly shouted a greeting.

"What's that you found?" she asked, bounding from the bike.

"Found the missing hound prints," Freddie boasted proudly.

Carly joined him at the water's edge, took a look at the prints, and announced that they were deer prints, not hound prints, and that Freddie should put his glasses back on.

"Are too hound prints," Freddie insisted.

"Are not," Carly stood behind her original interpretation.

Freddie put his glasses on, realized his mistake, but refused to admit it to his friend. Face flushed, he picked up his bike and headed down a path into the woods. Carly followed in close pursuit.

"I told you so," she sassed.

"Bring the candy bar you promised?" Freddie asked, changing the subject.

"Right here. One for me. One for you. But they're for later," she teased, patting a small vinyl pouch that served as a saddlebag. "If you're good."

The two friends rode in silence watching a red-tailed hawk making figure eights in the sky.

"I wonder if other hawks judge each other?" Freddie inquired.

"What?" Carly asked in amazement.

"You know, like figure skaters or gymnasts. Imagine a panel of six other hawks sitting in a tree holding up numbered cards judging that hawk's performance as it soars through the sky." Freddie's imagination was wild.

"You think of the weirdest things sometimes, Frederick." Carly called him Frederick when she was annoyed with him or when he began showing off his exceptional IQ.

Carly was in the lead now, pedaling as fast as her legs would pivot.

She knew exactly where she was taking her friend. They crossed familiar brooks and streams, passed trees that were turning colors and rode over damp mossy patches of lingering green.

"Smell that?" Freddie asked as they rounded a bend in the road. The pair lifted their noses to the air like well-trained tracking dogs.

"Could be somebody's wood stove," Carly offered.

"Seems a bit warm for a fire today, don't you think?" Freddie wasn't buying the wood stove explanation. "Maybe someone's burning leaves. Let's check it out."

Noses leading the way, the bicyclists turned onto a rocky

deer path that tested their mountain biking skills. Their handlebars twisted and turned at every crevice and large rock, but the pair kept peddling, finally reaching a grassy knoll, which gave them a bird's-eye view. In a thicket, beyond the next knoll, they could see a small trickle of smoke rising gently above the trees.

"Over there," Carly gulped, recognizing that part of the forest as the property of Strange Willie. "Grandpa wants me to stay away from there."

Freddie didn't hear the warning, as he was halfway down the hill, zeroing in on the source of the smoke.

"Could be someone's in trouble," he shouted back over his shoulder.

Carly had to make a choice, follow her friend or be left behind. She chose to follow him and glided smoothly down the path he had cut in the tall grass. She was panting heavily by the time she caught him at the edge of the opening in the trees.

"Shhhh," he said holding one finger across his lips to hush his friend.

"Look over there."

Carly looked and was shocked at the sight of Strange Willie sitting upright like a statue on his motorcycle, framed by the smoldering ruins of his burned-out trailer.

"Uh, oh," Freddie exclaimed. "There's that whacko, warvet who chases kids and boils them for dinner." He turned and started riding back through the forest, expecting Carly to be right at his heels. When he reached the clearing, he looked back over his shoulder and almost crashed into a

rock, when he realized Carly wasn't following him away from the danger.

Thinking his friend might have fallen, he turned around and retraced his steps. He stopped suddenly, almost biting his tongue, as he saw Carly bravely approaching the man on the motorcycle who appeared asleep. Like most children in today's ruthless society, he had been taught to avoid strangers, to talk to no adults no matter how friendly, and to be alert for oddball characters. Strange Willie had to be the strangest dude he'd ever seen.

"Still time to save this young girl who's been bitten by the crazy bug," he thought out loud. If only he could reach her before Strange Willie awoke and gobbled them both for dinner. It was not a pleasant thought. Perhaps it was too late already. In the distance, he could see Strange Willie stirring in the motorcycle seat.

"Look out," Freddie blurted at the top of his lungs.

Strange Willie also heard the shout and jerked the sleep from his head.

Startled, he reached for his shotgun and quickly aimed at the approaching figure still blurry in his vision. Nervous sweat formed on his brow, as the features of the small girl came into focus. His finger tightened on the trigger. Freddie held his breath. Carly stopped in her tracks and stared at the figure on the motorcycle. Once again she found herself out of breath. Speechless.

Strange Willie squinted until he recognized Carly. An upturned lip showed a slight smile as the muscles in his finger relaxed. As soon as Carly saw the smile, she knew the man, the same one who days earlier saved her life, was not to be feared. Freddie remained statue-like on his mountain bike, his breath coming in spasms. With a shaky hand, Freddie reached into his pocket and retrieved a small, plastic inhaler. The excitement brought on an asthma attack. He squirted the medicine in his mouth, took a deep breath, then exhaled. Slowly his lungs relaxed, the asthma released its grip on his body. He cautiously breathed a sigh of relief for himself, Carly, and the moment. But he remained motionless, waiting for a cue from his friend.

For several moments, Carly, Strange Willie, and Freddie did not move. The smoke continued to rise from smoldering embers deep within the trailer. Only the red fox, which was hiding a safe distance away, noticed Hampton inching his way down the trail, hopeful that it was safe to join the congregation. Strange Willie replaced his shotgun in a sling on the side of the motorcycle and Carly took this as a sign that she might approach the man. She dismounted, laid her bike on the ground, and walked slowly toward Strange Willie, still not sure what his reaction might be. He seemed more confused than when last they met. Shooting the skunk, he was confident, strong and proud. Now he seemed humbled, confused, even a bit scared. Carly noticed his left hand shake as he removed a dirty rag and wiped the sweat from his forehead. It left a brown smudge, like tracks in dirt accumulated over a lifetime. Ten feet from the man, Carly stopped and looked back over her shoulder. Freddie waved nervously from his vantage point. Confident, Carly took two steps closer. Strange Willie hung his head.

"You okay, Mister Willie?" Carly asked, not sure that she should call him by what all the folks in town did. Strange Willie might not know that people called him 'Strange Willie.'

Strange Willie did not answer. He lifted his head slowly, his eyes fixed on the ruins of his trailer home. Carly wasn't sure, but she thought she could see a tear illuminated by the sunlight as it rolled down his cheek. She turned her head and looked at the smoke rising from the pile of rubble. His pitiful home hadn't been much to begin with and now it was nothing. Strange Willie did not speak. There were no words needed to describe what both the man and child felt inside. Carly was experiencing, recognizing perhaps for the first time in her life, non-verbal communication. It was as though Strange Willie was talking to her without saying a word. She could feel his sadness, loneliness, emptiness. His desperation and his loss. Freddie, still on the hill, was not tuned in. He wanted to high tail it home, back to civilization, safety, and the Baby Ruth candy bars Carly had promised.

Carly and Strange Willie turned to face each other in unison. When their eyes met, Carly spoke, "You still have the motorcycle, Mister."

Strange Willie glanced back at the motorcycle, then at Carly, then back at the motorcycle. He squinted at Freddie. "The boy is not as brave as you," he said as clearly and eloquently as a television anchor.

"Oh, Freddie," Carly blushed wanting to protect the honor of her friend, "it's just, like he doesn't know you, that's all." She kicked dirt nervously with her left foot. "You know, I never had a chance to thank you the other day for saving my life and all."

"Did you thank your pony?" asked the man.

"Yes, yes, I did," answered Carly, still confused by his words.

"Then you thanked me enough," he replied. He blew his nose in the dirty rag.

Without asking, Carly took out one of the candy bars and handed it to the man who was sitting sidesaddle on the motorcycle, one leg slung over the fuel tank. He took the offering from the girl, ripped the wrapper, and ate it in two quick bites. Freddie's eyes popped wide. Acting strictly on instinct, he threw his bike on the ground and came screaming down the hill, no longer concerned with the safety of himself or Carly. In his haste, he tripped over a rusty chain concealed in the tall grass. He tumbled, landing at Carly's foot. For the first time, Strange Willie smiled. Carly, concerned for her friend, offered her hand, which Freddie quickly refused, his face red with embarrassment. As he watched the boy dust himself off, Strange Willie realized that the chocolate he had eaten probably had this boy's name on it.

"Greed," Strange Willie stated matter-of-factly. "It's what's turned the world upside down. Right from the start."

Freddie had absolutely no idea what this strange fellow was talking about. "What? What are you talking – greed?" Freddie had no clue.

"Never mind," Carly interrupted, "I'll explain later."

Strange Willie laughed again, swinging his leg as he dismounted from the motorcycle. Freddie took a frightened step back. Carly, feeling safe, remained where she was. The man walked past them and toward the blackened ruins of what was once his home. His refuge. He motioned with his body for his new companions to follow. They did. So did Hampton, who now had a clear shot at the remainder of his breakfast, out of his reach for many hours. Wisely, Hampton stayed in the shadows, a silent intruder not wanting to be discovered. His mission was simple. Get the chicken and get out.

Slowly, Strange Willie led the way back. The youngsters followed, Freddie's feet landing in the stranger's footprints. Twice he almost lost his balance. Freddie's antics were a welcome interlude in what was otherwise a somber situation. Carly grabbed her friend's arm as he fell a third time. Their eyes met for the first time since they had entered Strange Willie's fortress. Each child's eyes revealed their inner thoughts. Freddie's eyes, enlarged with curiosity, said, 'What's going on here?' Carly's eyes revealed emotional maturity well beyond her young years, soothing Freddie with an inviting, 'Trust me, friend, all is well.'

The smoke burned their eyes, soot covered their clothes, and ashes blackened their sneakers. Freddie kicked around in the debris, sending black puffs of smoke and ash into the already thick air. No words were needed to describe Strange Willie's feelings. The message was clear. They knew that once again fate, terrible and cruel, had sent Strange Willie crashing backwards toward tomorrow. Carly comprehended little of his world. Hers was one of security and love, even if her parents were thousands of miles away. The farm was her safe haven and grandfather provided an ample supply of love in his own way. There was always plenty to eat, warm heat when the wind blew cold, and the roof only leaked in a few places when it rained.

Now she was standing in Strange Willie's world or what was left of it. He had asked for very little in life – now what little he had was gone. Carly thought of those other abandoned men and women she had seen on the streets of Chicago when she visited her mom's parents. She wondered if that would be where Strange Willie would wind up. It made her shudder. He belonged out here in the mountains with the other wild creatures. A city would eat him. Devour him. In the wilderness she knew he could survive the coldest winter, the roughest terrain, the wildest weather. While fraught with danger, the backwoods were his home and refuge. The city presented other pitfalls, traps that would swallow him like quicksand, and squeeze his mind until it burst.

The trio kicked through the debris, careful not to re-kindle any smoldering embers. There was little left. A frying pan, a tin from a Christmas fruitcake twenty years ago, blackened springs from a mattress, and the charcoal remains of a bare light bulb suspended from a twisted metal rafter. Not much to show for sixty-three years of life on the planet. Strange Willie dug through a thick ash pile near what had been an old icebox. He looked like a coal miner emerging from the shafts, when he turned back toward Carly. Clutching a metal tin, he seemed to be saying, "All is okay. I will be fine." Freddie found an old can of marbles that was still too hot to hold. The top was propped open, revealing the treasure inside. Freddie looked over at Strange Willie and without hesitation Strange Willie nodded affirmatively to the boy. Later, Freddie would transfer the agates to his saddle pack and return home triumphantly, like the treasure seeker who found gold at the far side of a rainbow.

Rustling activity from the vicinity of the Harley Davidson motorcycle caught their attention. Swinging around, Strange Willie rushed to where his window had been, Carly close behind. In the fading sunlight, he could see Hampton retreating down the path with the chicken in his mouth. Carly shielded the sunlight from her eyes to see what was going on.

"That's Hampton, the missing hound from the Hunt." Before she could think about it the words were spewing from her mouth."

"My dawg!" Strange Willie said emphatically, his speech returning to the monotone, monosyllabic form he had adopted as part of his masquerade.

He had been playing this part for so long. In times of

social crises, this other personality took control.

"But that dog ..uh..hound...belongs to the Riverdale Hunt Club. It's been... " insisted Carly.

"No, my dawg," Strange Willie said stomping his foot, sending a cloud of ashes around his already blackened torso. He looked like a genie appearing in a magical cloud of smoke from a bottle. Carly almost laughed out loud, but sensed the mood had changed. There were things going on in Strange Willie's head that she clearly didn't understand.

"Whatever you say, Strange Willie." Oops! She said the

name out loud. Too late. No going back. She continued the sentence without pausing.

"It's your dog, if you say it is." She turned to Freddie. "Sun's getting low, Freddie, time we headed back. You know how fussy Grandpa Oakley is."

Sensing he was not going to be challenged, Strange Willie relaxed.

As they made their way carefully back to their bikes, Carly turned to wave good-bye. Strange Willie, standing in a column of soot, raised his left arm and returned the wave. His right hand still clutched the metal tin he had retrieved. Carly smiled, knowing in her heart that Strange Willie would be all right. For a while, anyway. As she and Freddie rode through the forest, they passed a satisfied hound finishing the last of his breakfast as the sun sank low in the sky. In the distance, she could hear Strange Willie whistling, calling the dog. Perhaps it really was his dog. Maybe she was mistaken.

Hounds do look alike. Carly wondered if she had to tell anybody that she'd found a missing hound. Of more concern was the fading sun, which was racing toward the horizon.

Their shortest route was to Freddie's house, where she could call her grandfather to pick her up. It was the only chance to save herself from being grounded for a week. Her grandfather would be grumpy, but he'd praise Carly for using her head and not staying out in the woods after dark.

Anyway, it was his turn to cook supper.

They never knew that Strange Willie followed them all the way to Freddie's street, watching over them so their journey would be safe.

CHAPTER 19

For the next few days, Carly and Freddie met regularly after school and biked into the woods to visit their friend. They brought him food, plastic bags, and even an old tent that, although punctured with holes, provided a makeshift home. The plastic bags adequately filled in the gaps. Each day was different, and they were careful not to stay too long. Sometimes they'd find Strange Willie asleep in the tent with the hound carefully guarding the entrance. They would leave

their gifts and ride away without waking their friend. Other times, he would share a candy bar with them. He rarely spoke. When he did, he told stories of the war, of bringing death and destruction to people with names he could not pronounce in a far-off land.

For several days they helped Strange Willie clean an area around the tent. Among their gifts were a winter coat and an old horse blanket Carly found in the hayloft. It was musty and old, but it could still provide warmth on bone-chilling winter nights.

Hampton was content living with Strange Willie who shared his meals with him. It seemed the hound was constantly hungry. Memories of the kennel, of his original home, were fading and he never wandered very far from the tent. Now and again, he could sense that they were being watched but never managed to see the fox that paid daily visits. And although the scent was strong on cold autumn mornings, he had no desire to give chase.

He had enough of being lost. There was newfound friendship in humans, the likes of which he had never experienced as a part of the pack. Those other humans had been kind to him, but there were just too many hounds for him to receive the individual attention he was getting now.

Carly caught a really bad cold, the flu perhaps, and her fever and coughing kept her out of school for two days. Freddie chose not to go into the woods alone. It was something the two friends shared and, besides, the days were getting very short. He didn't want to be caught alone in the forest after dark. On Thursday, Carly returned to class and over lunch she and Freddie discussed the need to check up on Strange Willie. The trouble was Grandpa Oakley had made it clear Carly needed extra rest, and that afterschool activities would be banned for a few more days. Carly persuaded Freddie to take the trip himself. She'd prepared a special bag of goodies for Strange Willie, and, while she would like to go, she had to stay home and miss the adventure. Reluctantly, Freddie agreed and the plain brown bag was passed from friend to friend. Riding home together, Carly reassured her buddy that everything would be fine. After all, they'd made the trip together dozens of times. All he'd have to do would be to ride in, say hello, drop off the bag, and ride out. Less than an hour.

"You can do it, Freddie," she coaxed as she skipped off the bus in front of Grandpa Oakley's mailbox.

"Wish me luck," he replied as the door closed, separating the two friends. Leaving a trail of lazy blue exhaust, the bus rolled on to its next stop.

"I'm sure that's great for my lungs and the Greenhouse Effect," Carly said, as she watched the yellow bus disappear over the rise. She really didn't know much about the Greenhouse Effect but was sure it was something else bad she'd have to worry about.

Her grandfather was out in the field mending fences, a farm chore that never seemed to end. He left a package of oatmeal cookies along with a note reminding his granddaughter to stay in and rest. Carly poured a glass of milk and plopped herself in front of the television. She hated watching television while the days were still warm, but she reluctantly obeyed her grandfather, since her coughing persisted and her full energy had not returned. She had enough strength to graze through the fifty channels on the cable television box. As the images flashed by, her mind wandered to the woods where she wondered how Freddie was doing. She wished he had a cellular telephone so he could report in. That only happens to kids on television, she thought, closing her eyes, and fell asleep.

The loud ring of the telephone awakened the sleeping girl. In the kitchen she could see her grandfather peeling carrots and putting them in a bowl. She loved carrots and often ate them for a snack. It kept her grandfather off her back when she refused to eat other vegetables that did not look appealing, like asparagus and cauliflower.Yuk.

"Get the phone, please." her grandfather called.

Carly picked up the telephone on the fourth ring. It was Mrs. Wheeler. Freddie's mom.

"No, no, he isn't, Mrs. Wheeler." Her grandfather listened from the kitchen but could only hear one side of the conversation. "I'm sure he'll be back soon. Yup, I'll call you if he comes by here. Yes, mam. I'll tell him to get his bu....ehhh...to get right home."

"What's up?" her grandfather asked as Carly hung up the phone. She was pale as a ghost.

"Uh, that was Freddie's mom. He's not home yet." She tried to sound calm. She sat in a yellow pool of light cast by a reading lamp beside the sofa. Outside, night had closed in and only a faint orange glow illuminated the sky. Inside, she knew Freddie was in trouble. But she couldn't say anything. Not yet.

Carly sat quietly throughout much of dinner. She toyed with her food, ate a few bites, then stared blankly at her plate. Her lack of appetite drew her grandfather's attention.

"Feeling under the weather still, Carly?" he asked as he cleaned his plate.

"I guess so, Grandpa. I had all those cookies before." It convinced the old man and he changed the subject, trying to engage his granddaughter in small talk. He did all the talking. Carly just sat and listened, every once in a while nodding in agreement. Finally, Grandpa Oakley gave up and sat quietly eating his rice pudding. Carly nibbled at the whipped cream. The silence was interrupted by the ringing of the telephone, which echoed through Carly's mind like the alarm at the firehouse.

"I'll get it," her grandfather said springing from the table. "Hello. Yes, good evening, Mrs. Wheeler," he said. Covering the mouthpiece, he whispered to Carly, "It's Freddie's mom." His attention turned back to the woman on the other end of the line. "No, mam. No sign of Freddie here.

What? No, I think you've waited long enough. Yes, I'd call them now.

We'll be right over. You stay calm."

Grandpa Oakley replaced the telephone receiver on the hook, took off his glasses, and rubbed his eyes. "Freddie's mom is frantic. The boy isn't home yet. I told her to call the Sheriff's office and that we'd be right over.

I've told you kids a million times to be home before dark. What a mess."

Carly swallowed hard without saying a word, retrieved a

winter coat from the closet, and zipped it up. It was getting cold out and she figured it was going to be a long night. Fingers crossed inside her coat pocket, she bounced onto the bench seat in the red Dodge pickup truck. The old man took a lantern, a flashlight, and an extra jacket, just in case. They drove in silence through the darkness, the inside of the cab illuminated only by the green control panel light which cast a ghostly pall across the two riders.

CHAPTER 20

It seemed every light in the Wheeler house was on as the red pickup turned into the driveway. The front door was open and, without knocking, Carly and her grandfather entered the split-level ranch. Built in the early '70's, the house was one of many homes Xeroxed in neat rows where farms once dotted the hillsides. Mrs. Wheeler lived in the three-bedroom home with her son. A daughter, Anne-Marie, was at college in Florida, and her ex-husband, Freddie's dad, had moved back to Washington, D.C. after the divorce.

Carly and her grandfather entered as Mrs. Wheeler hung up the telephone, her eyes red and puffy from crying. Within moments they learned that Freddie's dad, Jack Wheeler, would be there by ten o'clock and that the sheriff was sending a deputy to take the information about the missing boy.

A loud radio blasted in a distant room and the smell of

burned pot roast permeated the front hall. A cold breeze blew through the front screen door, which Freddie was supposed to have replaced with the storm door several weeks ago. The unusually warm autumn weather had extended his days of procrastination. Outside a distant Amtrak passenger train heading south whistled past a road crossing, as the deputy's police car pulled to a grinding stop on the Wheeler's gravel drive.

Hat in hand, the young law enforcement agent, Brian Webb, knocked on the screen door. He was a handsome man, twenty-four years old who had yet to outgrow his boyish appearance. His uniform was a size too big and hung loosely on his slender frame. He was polite, almost apologetic, as he greeted Freddie's distraught mother. Carly listened silently as the young man asked routine questions, pausing to pencil them in a spiral-bound pocket notepad. In between writing sentences, he would wet the end of the pencil with his lips, oblivious to the dangers of lead poisoning. Carly didn't understand how anyone could not know about the dangers of lead. She'd seen a television show on the educational channel about lead poisoning and had asked her grandfather about the paint in their home. He had reassured her that all was safe. Besides, she didn't go around eating paint chips now that she was no longer an infant. They shared a laugh knowing that lead poisoning was really no laughing matter. It was a lesson Carly would keep with her the rest of her life.

The boy's height, weight, and what he was wearing when he left home were all carefully chronicled in the notebook. Brian Webb took great notes and for this had already been commended by his superiors during his short tenure with the force. After questioning Mrs. Wheeler, the Sheriff's deputy turned to Grandpa Oakley who couldn't fill in any more details. From the corner of his eye, Brian Webb noticed Carly moving restlessly in the reclining chair that she had managed to push back to its most horizontal position. She was fighting to bring the chair upright again, but it was fighting back.

"And what about you, young lady?" The question was direct. With one final effort, Carly flung the chair back to its upright position, a move that nearly catapulted her across the floor. She managed just in time to catch her balance and landed at the officer's feet. He was at least two feet taller than Carly, and she had to strain her neck to see his face. She realized the trouble Freddie might be in and that time was not on her side. She looked at her grandpa, at Mrs. Wheeler, and at Brian Webb who now stooped at her side. They were eye to eye. Before she knew it, the entire story of the past two weeks came streaming from her memory. Carly recalled the smallest details and told a tale that was bizarre, alarming, yet totally believable. She was careful not to omit any pertinent clues. Freddie's life depended on her accuracy.

An hour later she repeated the story to the sheriff and a throng of television and newspaper reporters who had been monitoring the police scanner. This was big news in an area where stories usually came from other parts of the world. The quiet scene, which began with just Mrs. Wheeler, Grandpa Oakley, Carly, and Officer Webb, was now alive with the buzz of several dozen people. Upon hearing her story, the deputy notified his boss, Sheriff Jerome Homestack, who left an unfinished dinner and a screaming baby, driving at top speed to the Wheeler home. Other calls to relatives and friends brought immediate response. A State police helicopter landed in a nearby field and the pilot received instructions

from Grandpa Oakley who knew the area better than anyone, having lived there for nearly seven decades. Carly sat at the dining room table, twisting a braid between her thumb and index finger while she told and retold the story. The television lights made her squint and every few seconds a flash from a still camera brightened the room. Mrs. Wheeler's sister, Terry, made coffee for everyone and tried to comfort the distraught mother of the missing boy. Freddie's father arrived and was told that a ground search of the area was about to begin. The helicopter would fly over the more remote areas because no one, except Carly, seemed to know exactly where Strange Willie's trailer was located. An all-points bulletin with a detailed description of Strange Willie was dispatched on the police radios. Carly gave them the best directions she knew to his trailer. She knew by heart the path she and Freddie followed on their bicycles, but she was at a loss to accurately describe it to the search team. The oak tree with the gnarled branch, where they always took a shortcut, was not on any map.

An hour later, the helicopter pilot radioed back that he had flown over what appeared to be a burned-out trailer deep in the woods but hadn't seen any sign of life. Police cars continued patrolling the back roads but sending a rescue team into the dark woods at night would be useless. Shortly after midnight, it was decided that an all-out search would begin at daybreak. There had been no sightings of Strange Willie or the boy. In the midst of the continuing commotion, Carly lay asleep on the living room couch. Her teacher, a college friend of Mrs. Wheeler, had placed an afghan over the sleeping child.

Carly tried her best to stay awake, to answer any more questions anyone might have. She actually enjoyed being in the spotlight, all the while terrified that her friend might be in real danger. Just before falling asleep, she tried contacting Freddie with mind thoughts. But there was no answer. Perhaps she was over-tired. Perhaps Freddie didn't know how to answer. The mental exercise was exhausting. Her brain turned off and she found refuge in sleep.

CHAPTER 21

The first slivers of light were creeping over the mountains. At first Carly didn't remember where she was. Her grandfather shook her gently. In the Wheeler house twice as many people as there had been the night before scurried around, and the young girl quickly realized the situation hadn't changed. News footage with Carly's face flickered on a television set from across the room. Handheld walkie-talkie radios crackled. Two portable cellular telephones rang simultaneously, and the shrill sounds of a whistling teapot pierced the air. Outside the activity was even more frantic. The driveway pulsated with constantly moving vehicles, including an occasional police car with sirens blasting. Several horse trailers were parked in the lot across the street, with horses and their riders ready to assist in the search for the missing boy. A large mobile home with a dozen radio antennae was stationed at the foot of the driveway. From this command station, Sheriff Jerome Homestack directed the entire operation. Printed sheets with Freddie's picture and description were handed out to the growing number of volunteer searchers gathered on this once tranquil street in a rural Virginia town.

Carly rubbed the sleep from her eyes. As she sat up, her grandfather handed her a mug of hot chocolate. Tiny white marshmallows floated in the velvety liquid. Deputy Webb debated loudly with a local television reporter who wanted to interview Carly live on the eye-opener news. The police officer had strict instructions to keep all media on the lawn, out of the house. The reporter did not like the answers he was getting, but Deputy Webb had his feet planted firmly on the welcome mat just outside the door. During the night, someone replaced the screen with the proper storm door panels, keeping the cold night wind where it belonged, outside.

Carly noticed her grandfather holding her riding boots and chaps, the leather leggings that she wore over her jeans. The youngster was not exactly sure why her grandfather was standing there with her riding clothes. In the brightening dawn, she saw a familiar sight on the lawn, her grandfather's horse trailer with Monroe tethered to the side. Mr. Briggs, the stable master at the Hunt, was tightening the pony's girth. The riding clothes. The pony. The picture became clear. She was going to lead a search party through the woods to show officials the way to Strange Willie's.

From the living room, she overheard conversations she didn't like.

Stories that were untrue. People pointed a finger at

Strange Willie, convinced he was behind Freddie's disappearance. In her heart she knew this wasn't the case. If anything, Strange Willie would help find the missing boy. Didn't anyone know he was a hero? Didn't anyone know that? She remembered the story Strange Willie told her about heroism and how he wasn't interested in rewards or medals. He didn't need or want the recognition. So how could anyone know? Strange Willie kept his deeds of heroism to himself. And now his silence was turning against him. If only the people knew. Carly was about to explode. She wanted to shout, to tell everyone that they were all wrong about Strange Willie.

Unexpectedly, she felt a gentle hand on her shoulder. "It's getting late, Carly. Time to get ready," her grandfather said as he pushed her toward a bedroom where she could change her clothes. Outside a loudspeaker blared, calling everyone's attention to the center of what was becoming a media circus.

Moments later, after quickly downing a bowl of hot cereal, Carly dashed outside to where Monroe waited. An army of fifty volunteers marched down the road, fanning out to search a nearby farm. Another twenty men and women drove to strategic points on the other side of the highway where in groups of five or six they searched nearby trails. Two state police helicopters and one television helicopter flew in formation overhead, then buzzed off in different directions. Everywhere Carly saw volunteers on motorcycles, mountain bikes, and on foot. Cars and trucks of all shapes and sizes, some with only a driver, others packed with seven or eight people captured her attention. A young boy was missing and the surrounding community responded to the call.

Rumors were flying everywhere. Someone said they had seen a boy tied up in the back of a station wagon headed North on I-95. Another report claimed Freddie was seen climbing aboard a boxcar in the freight yards.

The most outrageous story had the young boy floating down the river in a homemade wooden canoe. Each story grew out of some truth but none had any real relationship to Freddie or his whereabouts.

Carly led the parade of six horses as it ventured out along the path leading from the Wheeler's cul-de-sac. She and

Freddie followed this route on their mountain bikes a million times and she knew it by heart. Rarely used these days as a horse trail, it proved difficult for the equestrians as their mounts stumbled over roots and debris. Looking back, Carly couldn't believe the procession she was leading. Her life had taken some odd twists in the last few weeks and now she was heading a search party for her dearest friend, missing over twelve hours. She looked around in awe at the others in the group. There was Jack Tidbit and Missy Mandell, the two top whips for the Riverdale Hunt. Master Drury had sent special orders for as many hunt members as possible to join the search. A few miles away he and twenty other volunteers on a similar mission searched a trail east of the Wheeler house. Elsewhere, a dozen other search and rescue parties branched out in all directions, like the spokes of a wheel.

With steady precision, Carly's small band journeyed deeper into the forest she affectionately called "Bullfrog Gulch." Even now with winter rehearsing its icy chills, bullfrogs could be heard serenading the riders as they trotted along. Following closely behind Monroe were two mounted state police officers whose names Carly couldn't remember. Right behind them were the two whips whose skill on these wooded trails was unsurpassed. Bringing up the rear was Grandpa Oakley riding his old mule, Hardtack, who many years earlier pulled the aging farmer's plow. Despite his age, the thirty-two-year-old mule still provided a steady platform for the old man. The mule even had an occasional buck in him. Carly hoped he was in good enough condition for this long, arduous journey.

Keeping a steady pace, Carly's crew walked the first mile, the footing underneath treacherous. Where the path crossed a brook at the old mill, the horses picked up a steady trot. Carly kept her pony moving straight ahead, while older members of the caravan split away, searching trails that branched left and right. Finding no signs of the missing boy, they turned around and sprinted back to Carly before they lost track of her. The old mule carrying her grandfather plodded along determined to do his share in this time of crisis. While Carly was pleased to see old Hardtack keeping up, her grandfather did not smile as he bounced along. He couldn't remember the last time he was in the saddle. It seemed a lifetime away.

The cold night left a skim of ice on shallow ponds and morning sunlight made the ice crystals dance as the parade of horses marched by.

Carly's head was a swirl of emotions. Remorse, for tormenting Freddie until he agreed to bring the relief package to Strange Willie. By himself. Guilt, for not telling Mrs. Wheeler where Freddie had gone the first time she called. Honor, for telling the whole story once she realized the real trouble she had caused. And finally, pride, for being chosen leader of such an honorable delegation. The last two emotions made her feel better, so Carly decided to stick with them. After all, there would be time for apologies later. Sitting straight and tall in the saddle she was very business-like as she led the group further away from civilization.

They rode quietly for a time, until the roar of a helicopter skimming nearby treetops shattered the silence. One police horse reared, others acted jittery, prancing and snorting. The blades of the helicopter sent a hurricane of wind over the riders and blinded them with swirling leaves, dirt and pine needles. The taller state trooper, Sterling Bixby, the one with the mustache, yelled into his radio, and, in a few seconds, the helicopter lifted up and away from the horses. Temporarily blinded, Carly wiped dirt from her eyes, stroked Monroe's long neck to calm him, then continued trotting along the well-worn trail, the group in close pursuit. She was sure the house trailer, Strange Willie, and perhaps even Freddie were just over the next hill. What she didn't know was what awaited them over that hill.

In the overnight excitement, all thoughts of Hampton had been pushed aside. For one, Carly had forgotten about the missing hound. As far as Carly was concerned, the 'Dawg', as she liked to mimic, was Strange Willie's pet.

In fact, Carly didn't think of Hampton as missing anymore. Wherever Strange Willie went, right by his side was the hound, or dog, or 'Dawg,' whatever he was called. Hampton totally accepted Strange Willie as his master and Strange Willie adopted Hampton as his friend. Only to Strange Willie he wasn't called Hampton anymore, he was called just plain 'Dawg'.

Hidden by the underbrush, Hampton sensed the equestrians long before they topped the hill and, wagging his tail, rushed out to meet them. At first sight, the two whips sang out in unison, "Hampton. It's Hampton. We've found Hampton."

The hound recognized the hunt staff members and wiggled excitedly, eager for their attention. Just beyond Hampton

lay the blackened ruins of Strange Willie's fortress exactly as Carly had described it. Despite being forewarned, it was a shock to their senses. The state police officers dismounted, and, with guns drawn, started toward the ruins, paying no attention to Hampton who circled them frantically. Distraught, Carly pleaded with the troopers to put their guns away, insisting that Strange Willie wouldn't harm anyone. The younger trooper, Randy Scudder, on edge at having never removed his gun from his holster before, brushed aside the young girl's plea.

"You did a great job getting us here," he glared at Carly, pushing her away with his eyes. "We'll take over. The rest of you get back out of the way. Somebody get this mutt away from me." Hampton jumped at his leg trying to divert his attention.

While the others watched a safe distance away, the two troopers crouched low, edging their way down the hill toward the ash pile.

Carly held her breath then let out a giant sigh of relief. The taller trooper turned around and put his finger to his lips, warning Carly to keep quiet.

What she noticed took all the tension out of the moment and she wanted to share her discovery with the others. Strange Willie's motorcycle and makeshift tent were gone. Carly whistled. The officers turned at Carly's whistle, angry she had disobeyed. Now she was on her feet shouting at the troopers.

"Strange Willie, ain't here!!!" she blurted out.

"Carly," her grandfather admonished. "use isn't, not ain't, dear." She couldn't believe her grandfather was being so grammatically correct at a time like this.

"What are you saying, young lady," the mustached trooper asked, ignoring the old man's idle remarks.

"Strange Willie, ain't—uh—isn't here," she repeated glancing at her grandfather for approval. It came back in the form of a quiet nod from the elder gentleman. "See over there beyond where the trailer once stood?" Everyone looked. "Well, that's where he always kept his motorcycle, a Harley chopper," she smiled. "And besides, we helped him make a tent to sleep in after the trailer burned. Look around. Can anyone see a tent anywhere around here?"

Not believing her, although feeling less nervous, the officers continued toward the trailer. They no longer crouched. Meanwhile, Missy Mandell and Jack Tidbit, the whippers-in, knelt next to Hampton whose excitement couldn't be contained. They tried calming him down but his dance continued. Puzzled by his behavior, Carly watched the hound's antics. She had developed a keen awareness of animal behavior and something was telling her that Hampton was more than just excited to see his former handlers.

"He's trying to tell us something," Carly realized, flailing her arms.

Like the hound, she needed everyone's immediate attention. "I think he wants us to follow him."

"The girl's right," said the younger officer as he returned from the trailer. Their search had uncovered nothing except the ashes of an empty life.

Jack Tidbit slipped a leather collar around Hampton's neck and held him at the end of a six-foot leash. The frantic animal pulled and strained, kicking dirt with his front paws as he tried to get away. Not understanding why he was collared, Hampton let out a howl. Carly realized Hampton would be returned to the hunt kennel, taken away from Strange Willie, no matter what happened today. Saddened, she pushed the thought out of her mind and urged the whip to release the hound. It wasn't necessary.

With determination, the hound ran toward the whip, then changed direction suddenly, yanking the leash out of Jack Tidbit's hand. Hoping someone would get the message and follow him, Hampton charged down the path and across a meadow. Triumph. Without further delay, the group remounted and chased the hound at full speed. It didn't take long to catch Hampton and soon the whippers-in rode at his heels like in a real hunt. Obligingly, Carly gave up her position as lead rider and was content just to be part of the chase. As they galloped, she wondered where the hound was taking them and if there'd be any jumps along the way. She hoped there would be.

Unseen by everyone, a certain red fox led the way, three-quarters of a mile down the road. A small cloud of dust rose in the early morning light as the equestrians raced across the field. Only the fox and hound knew their destination.

CHAPTER 22

The mobile radios blared louder than ever carrying news from state police Helicopter One. A man was spotted riding a Harley chopper down an old logging road leading away from Jackson Morgan's hunting cabin. They were in pursuit. A second helicopter joined the chase and several riders on all-terrain vehicles, other riders on horseback, closed in. Sheriff Homestack held three portable radios alternately listening and talking into each one.

From his command post miles away, he orchestrated the high-speed chase through woods he could not see. He was adept at his job, able to juggle several conversations at once. When he spoke, the sentences were short, direct, and easy to understand. A mix-up, a misunderstanding, could be disastrous.

Grazing the treetops, the helicopters closed in on the fleeing motorcycle as it sped along the forest floor. Memories of being chased through the jungles of Vietnam raced through Strange Willie's brain. This wasn't the first time he was running for his life. Only difference now he was being pursued by his own army. The past and present were jumbled in his brain. He felt the pressure building. He was racing into a black hole. There was no escape. Feeling numb, he slowed down the motorcycle, then stopped. The helicopters hovered ominously overhead. Clasping his hands behind his head in the universal posture of surrender, Strange Willie sat down by the edge of the road and gave up. A small tin container, blackened by soot, peeked out from his tattered leather jacket.

At the Wheeler house there was shouting and clapping as news of the capture filtered back over the radio. Strange Willie would lead them to Freddie. Or so everyone thought.

CHAPTER 23

The fox left a very distinct trail that was easy for Hampton to follow as he led the pack of horses, one mule and six riders, across the wooded trails. Carly felt comfortable in the saddle, passing landmarks forever etched in her young mind. Monroe, her brave pony, held his sparkling white tail straight out as he proudly galloped along the trail. The miles swept under his paws as Hampton led them over streams, past meadows, and through decaying forests. His stride was even and true, neither slowing down nor speeding up. Over the police radios, the group learned the news of Strange Willie's capture. Carly pushed it out of her mind, knowing her priority was to find her friend and deal with the lies about Strange Willie later. She knew there was a logical explanation. For now, that answer lay hidden in the deep foliage, which also masked the secrets of Freddie's whereabouts. At each bend, Carly envisioned seeing her friend's bubbly face with his warm smile greeting the search party. But at each turn, there was just another empty trail, another endless road to follow.

At the top of a knoll where the trees knelt by a meadow, Hampton stopped to catch his breath. He was panting heavily from the long distance run. He glanced back toward the small group of riders making sure they were still close behind. A small dust cloud assured him they were. The fox too had stopped to rest. In the distance the long, low rumble of an approaching storm bounced off outlying mountains. Monroe's ears pitched forward as he listened to an unseen animal rustling through the forest. Carly noticed the dark clouds forming in the distance. While it was highly unusual for a thunderstorm so late in the season, on occasion Mother Nature would break her own rules and send lighting, thunder, and often hail, crashing from the heavens. These quick storms were followed by much colder temperatures, ushered in on gale-force northwest winds. Carly was glad she wore her warm jacket and leather chaps. She turned her thoughts away from the oncoming storm and back toward Hampton who was circling frantically, his loud bark beckoning the small posse. With a wave of her hand, Carly acknowledged the hound's urging and moved Monroe in his direction. Hampton whirled and darted down the trail again.

Having regained the lead, Monroe panted heavily, gasping for more oxygen as the chase led up a steep hill. A short distance ahead, a wooden, crudely made platform bridged a gully at the highest point on the trail. Carly and Freddie had discovered the makeshift bridge spanning a stream as a shortcut home, and they often rode their bikes over this fragile structure. Over the months, weather rotted the wood and each crossing of a bicycle or motorcycle further weakened the timbers. As they raced toward the bridge, Monroe's ears pitched forward in alarm. Carly immediately saw the danger and pulled hard on the reins. The pony came to a sliding halt as did the two state police officers and the two whips. Unfortunately, Grandpa Oakley's mule, who had finally gotten enough energy to run up the hill, couldn't stop in time, and plowed into the back of the large Morgan horse the trooper rode. There was a flurry of dust and kicking heels. The mule lurched forward and threw Grandpa to the ground. Carly didn't hear the commotion behind her. She was mesmerized by the splintered remains of the bridge. Only a single log remained in place. The rest of the boards and plywood had fallen and crashed one hundred feet below. Hampton, now a champion of the forest, without hesitation, danced smartly across the one remaining log. When he reached the far side, he turned to see if the group was following. How could he know there was no way a horse or pony could tightrope walk across the log? Impatiently, he treaded anxiously in place.

From where Carly sat on her pony, she couldn't see into the gully.

Her grandfather, who had brushed himself off, limped slightly leading the mule forward, slowly, reluctantly, past Carly toward the foot of what remained of the bridge. Reaching the edge, Grandpa Oakley nervously looked down to the bottom. He whistled lowly to himself, his eyes focused on a tangled metal object lying near the stream. It was a bicycle. The twisted remains of a mountain bike.

When Freddie rode his battle-ship gray, two-wheeler over the bridge it collapsed sending the rider and bicycle careening down the steep slope.

Grandfather Oakley was sure it was the boy's bike. Freddie frequently rode it at the Oakley farm and the old man had seen it often enough to know there was no mistake. This was Freddie's bike. Trembling, Carly joined her grandfather and one look into the gully sent more shivers through her body. She brought her hands to her eyes in panic, scraping the buckle of her reins against her cheek. A small red line appeared, but she was too numb to feel the pain. How much trouble had she caused already? She had dared Freddie to go into the woods alone. Now the bridge lay in ruins. How many times had she ridden over it? It seemed so safe, although it squeaked and wheezed every time she made the crossing. What she didn't know was that Strange Willie had found the shortcut and regularly drove his motorcycle over it. The weight of the Harley was too heavy for the makeshift bridge and had weakened the structure.

Word of the wrecked bicycle raced through the small search party. Within seconds the two officers, using a rope carried on the saddle for this very purpose, repelled the steep cliff. Branches and chipped rocks became ladder rungs, as the troopers lowered themselves. Exhausted, they jumped the final six feet onto the rocky ledge of the streambed, landing within yards of the crumpled mountain bike, wedged, between two boulders. Next to it dangling on a broken twig was a hat. A baseball cap with a large red "F" above the brim. Freddie's hat. His logo. His trademark. The boy never went anywhere without the hat worn backwards, except in church where the pastor admonished him to take it off or lose it. No Freddie.

Once again, at the top of the ravine, Hampton barked for his friends to follow. The red fox paced back and forth across the wooded trail just out of sight. Even he was perplexed by the unexpected stop at the broken bridge.

What Hampton and the fox knew, but couldn't share with the humans, was that Freddie was another mile down the trail. And time was running out.

As the whips led the police horses, Carly guided the remaining riders down a rocky trail, which descended into the gully. It was a fifteen-minute ride down one side of the steep hill to where the trail met the streambed at a landing thick with rushes. It was a short ride along the water's edge to where the bike had fallen. The group was silent, grim about what they might find. Rounding a bend, they saw the wreck-

age, a heap of twisted metal, as though some sculptor had created a gruesome piece of modern art. Could Freddie have faired any better? In nearby undergrowth the officers searched for the boy's body. Carly dismounted and led

Monroe closer to the fallen bike. She picked up the baseball cap holding it in both hands. Her thoughts raced frantically, just slightly slower than her heart.

Then a strange thing happened. Her mind went blank. Where there had been a kaleidoscope of sights and sounds, now there was only white light. She heard no sounds. And from within the white light there appeared a shadow. It was Freddie and he was safe. He was in a structure that Carly had trouble seeing clearly. It was an old structure. A house made of logs. In an instant the mental picture burst. It appeared for only a fraction of a second, but the message was clear. She knew exactly where Freddie was. She must alert the others.

"Freddie's not here!" Carly shouted. "Freddie's not here!"

"What's that, Carly?" Grandpa Oakley questioned, as the group circled the young girl whose instincts they had come to trust.

Carly swallowed hard trying to dislodge the lump in her throat. Her lips were dry. "Freddie's not here," she repeated. "I think I know where he is."

"How could you know this?" questioned the younger officer.

"I don't know how. I just do. I just do," Carly pleaded, not wanting to tell anyone that she had seen Freddie in a corner of her imagination, a part of her mind she just recently learned to explore. Enough time had been spent here at the gorge.

"Is he okay?" asked Jack Tidbit, the whip who had heard only a portion of the conversation.

"I don't know that. But I just know where he is. Follow

me," Carly said excitedly, as she swung onto her pony and headed back down the path next to the stream.

Without further questions, the group quickly remounted and followed Carly who was already two hundred yards away. High overhead on the ledge, Hampton watched the group heading out, then turned and raced off on his own. He knew Carly would lead them to Freddie. He would meet them there. The red fox sensed the renewed activity and was safely on his way toward the rendezvous at the log cabin. Freddie and Carly had discovered the abandoned log cabin and it became their hiding place, a secret that they shared with no one, not even their friends at school. They feared that word of their find would reach the adults who would declare it off limits to the young explorers.

Located a little more than a mile away from where the bicycle fell, it took the search party less than six minutes to reach. Where the land was open, Carly rode at a full gallop, but where the trail wound tightly through the forest, she kept Monroe at a fast trot. This wooded trail was notorious as a knee-banger, as it wove in and around the trees. Cutting a corner too closely meant a sure collision between rider and tree trunk. Carly had come home with more than a few black and blue marks or battered shins having done battle with the trees. Now she rode carefully, dodging each obstacle like a seasoned slalom skier. Unfortunately, Hardtack the mule wasn't as agile and Grandpa Oakley smashed his knees into several tree trunks, grimacing with each collision.

Hampton arrived at the log cabin and was waiting on the porch as the group trotted out of the woods and into the clearing in front of the abandoned structure. Officer Sterling Bixby rode behind Carly and was the second to see the log cabin, as the forest unveiled its hiding place.

"Wait, no, don't go in there!" he shouted at the girl who was already on the ground running toward the cabin. She either didn't hear or didn't want to hear because she neither stopped nor looked back, as she vaulted onto the porch. Hampton darted in and out of the door, which swung on two rusted, but recently repaired hinges. Carly remembered that the door had hung precariously from one broken hinge last time she and Freddie played here. Old rags, newly stuffed into holes in the walls, kept out the relentless wind.

Inside, in the dim light, she saw an old mattress wedged against the far wall covered by the old horse blanket she had given to Strange Willie.

There was something or somebody huddled under the blanket. Fearful, Carly planted her feet, the floor creaking under her muddy paddock boots. She had successfully led the search party this far. Brave as she was, she was still only eleven years old and knew an adult should take over. Carly turned to call one of the adults into the cabin and was nearly knocked over by the troopers as they rushed by her. Stammering, she pointed toward the faded green horse blanket that she thought concealed Freddie. Of this she was certain. What she didn't know was the condition of her friend.

Officer Randy Scudder reached the bed first and without hesitation gently pulled the blanket aside revealing the motionless form. A dirty bandage wrapped around Freddie's head, the boy lay unconscious; a quick check showed a strong pulse and normal breathing. The trooper reached for his two-way radio, and, in between gasps for air, radioed his report back to Sheriff Jerome Homestack who was awaiting word in his command trailer.

A police helicopter with a doctor and nurse were whirling toward the abandoned cabin within seconds of the radio transmission.

After being told that he was alive, Carly mustered the courage to look at her injured friend. His once joyful face was now expressionless, the color gone from his complexion. As she gazed caringly, Carly felt the air grow very dense in the room. She turned away, ran out the door onto the porch, and sat on the top step. Hampton came over, sat down, and licked her face. Tears rolled down her cheeks, but she wasn't really crying. Hampton tasted the salty tears and wondered why the young girl was so sad. Hadn't she led the search party to her friend and wasn't help now on the way? What Hampton didn't realize was the heavy weight she carried on her young shoulders, a burden that would linger until she knew her friend was out of danger. Hampton stopped licking her cheek and looked up at Grandpa Oakley, who was standing beside his granddaughter. He gave the hound a pat on the head as he sat down next to Carly, putting his arm around her. She leaned her head into her grandfather's shoulder and cried softly. He stroked her hair.

"You did a fine job, Carly. You know, you probably saved your friend's life. You're a hero." The words rang empty in her head, which swirled with other images and thoughts. She remembered what Strange Willie had told her about being a

hero. She didn't want to be any kind of hero. She just wanted Freddie to be okay. If only she could go back to yesterday, she would tell Freddie not to go into the woods alone. If only she could go back to last summer when she and Freddie built the bridge, she would tell Freddie that the bridge wasn't a good idea and not to build it. But her yesterdays were locked away, out of reach. She longed to shrink into her warm, protective bed and pull the covers over her head. Her thoughts were drowned by the roar of the medical helicopter, soaring over the treetops.

Medical help had arrived for Freddie. Hovering overhead, with nowhere to safely land, the crew lowered a doctor in a wire harness. Meeting him on the ground, the older officer unhooked the harness and led the medic to the injured boy. Carly sat outside the cabin, comforted by her grandfather, as the white-gowned doctor examined Freddie. It seemed to take forever. The helicopter waited just above the treetops, its blades creating storm-like winds on the ground below. Finally the doctor emerged smiling. The news was encouraging. Freddie had a concussion, but his heart and other vital signs were good. No broken bones. He was still unconscious.

The two officers carried out the boy's limp body still wrapped in the old horse blanket. They carefully strapped him to a stretcher and radioed to the pilot, who expertly lifted the delicate package up to a waiting emergency medical technician in the helicopter. Holding her ears, Carly watched her friend as he was hoisted into the air. The noise from the helicopter was deafening. Freddie had always wanted to ride in a 'copter' as he called it. Too bad he wouldn't remember today's ride.

Once again, the harness for the doctor was dropped and seconds later the white form rose ghost-like into the air. As she watched the event unfold, Carly was unaware that Hampton sat by her side, resting his chin in her lap.

She covered her eyes as the helicopter lifted skyward kicking dirt, rocks and leaves in all directions. As quickly as it had come, the helicopter was out of sight, the roar of its engine and whirling blades fading into the distance as it rushed her friend toward the hospital twenty miles away. She was amazed how quickly the sound vanished as though someone had faded the volume down and off. Where once the helicopter roared, there were only the serene sounds of the forest. Overhead, a squawking flock of Canada geese passed on their way south.

Carly looked up and saw the first flakes of snow falling. The weather had turned cold quickly and Carly shivered. She zippered her coat. There were so many unanswered questions. She could see them on the faces of the others in the group as they chatted in small clusters. Carly couldn't hear what they were saying but it was written in their eyes. The same questions swam through her brain. How had Freddie managed to get from the gully to the house? It was more than a mile. Had he walked on his own or had Strange Willie found him and carried him to the house? If that were the case, why hadn't Strange Willie come for help? Why had he run away? And what would they do to Strange Willie?

"Time to go, Carly," her grandfather said softly. At first she didn't hear. "Let's go, sweetheart, before the snow gets too heavy."

Carly was only slightly aware of moving from the porch and mounting her pony who had found a stubble of grass on which to dine. All of the horses, as well as the mule, were busy eating as the search party re-mounted and headed home. Whether anyone spoke or if they rode in silence, Carly did not know for sure. The same questions raced through her brain, blocking out her other senses. She knew the way home and guided the group without thinking about what was she doing. She wasn't aware that Hampton accompanied the group home, a red collar around his neck tethered by a rope to the strong hands of Missy Mandell, the whip. Finding the missing hound was an added bonus, and now he was on his way home where he belonged.

Hampton wasn't given the option of staying in the woods. Carly didn't realize this, as she rode in silence at the head of the group. Not noticed by anyone was the red fox that watched the procession from a vantage point on a nearby boulder.

CHAPTER 24

Snow fell heavily. The search groups slowly filtered back into the Wheeler yard. A sense of relief replaced the frantic pace of a few hours ago. People smiled, laughed, and joked, as they exchanged stories and information. Strange Willie was not smiling. He sat locked in the back seat of a police cruiser. His treasured motorcycle remained in the woods at the place where Strange Willie surrendered, the snow silently piling on the bike, as it lay abandoned on its side. He had not been told that Freddie had been found or that the young boy, at this very moment, was being flown to Mercy Hospital. In fact, no one had spoken to the disheveled man for more than an hour.

They had given him a cup of coffee and a blanket that he wore tightly wrapped around his shoulders, then left him alone. The heat was not running in the car and the temperature had dropped dramatically. He shivered.

Mr. and Mrs. Wheeler were on the way to the hospital to meet their son. It was the first trip they shared in more than a half-dozen years since Mr. Wheeler moved to the Capitol district. Mrs. Wheeler watched the countryside pass. Mr. Wheeler looked at his ex-wife with a sense of compassion he hadn't experienced in years. He reached out and took her hand. At first, the woman withdrew her hand, then warmly put it back in his and squeezed gently. She looked at him through tearful eyes and managed a slight smile that he returned. They sat in silence for the rest of the journey.

Carly guided her rescue group expertly back through woods and onto the trail leading to Freddie's house, where a large cheer greeted them as they trotted up the driveway. Jumping from her exhausted pony, she gave the reins to Mr. Briggs who waited with Monroe's halter and lead line. The reporters with television cameras and lights descended on Carly, but before they could ask her any questions, Deputy Sheriff Brian Webb whisked her into the house. He waved his hand at the reporters telling them to let the young girl through, she was wet and tired and would be available for questions later. Carly was thankful for the protection the young lawman afforded, since she didn't want to speak to anyone. Not just yet. Out of the corner of her eye, she spotted Strange Willie sitting alone locked in the police cruiser. His hollow eyes looked vacant as though it were only his body sitting in the back seat. They could never take his soul Carly thought.

As the door to the Wheeler house closed, she saw Strange Willie look up, but then he was out of sight.

"What are you going to do with Willie?" Carly wanted to know.

"Never mind that right now," replied her grandfather as he joined her in the kitchen, his joints stiff from the long ride on Hardtack, his leg sore from the fall. "The sheriff'll take care of him, I'm sure. Imagine, finding that boy and not telling anybody about it!"

"Willie saved him," protested Carly.

"Sure, sweetheart, whatever you say. Let's get you out of your wet clothes before you end up in the hospital next to your friend."

Carly was too tired to protest and besides she knew it wouldn't do any good. Strange Willie could take care of himself and shortly everyone would know he was a hero, as soon as Freddie woke up and told the real story.

Carly took a hot shower and changed into a fresh pair of jeans, a flannel top and sweatshirt. The dry socks and sneakers warmed her feet.

There was hot chocolate and good news waiting for her when she rejoined the group in the kitchen. A phone call from the hospital reported that Freddie had woken up, and, except for a headache, was feeling much better. The only trouble was he couldn't remember anything after he started out across the wooden bridge. His mind was a blank from that point until he woke up in the hospital where his mother and father greeted him from the foot of the bed. He didn't even remember riding across the bridge, the accident, or how he got to the log cabin where he was rescued. Reporters were milling about the hospital waiting room eager to have the boy re-tell his story. Only he couldn't remember the story.

At the Wheelers, a second group of reporters gathered in the living room where Sheriff Homestack read a prepared statement. After he spoke, Carly told of her adventure then answered questions for more than hour, being careful not to portray herself as the hero. She didn't like the attention, and, all the while she spoke, wondered about the fate of Strange Willie.

Back in the kitchen she overheard the two state police officers talking with Deputy Webb. She didn't like what she was hearing. They laughed as they spoke of the crazy, deranged man and how he had refused to talk about the boy or answer questions about how Freddie ended up at the cabin covered with a horse blanket. As far as the police were concerned, and this came all the way from the top, the strange fellow had left Freddie in the cabin to die.

No way of knowing the truth. Strange Willie wasn't talking and Freddie couldn't remember any of the details. Hampton the hound and the red fox were the only other witnesses to his heroic deeds. No one would ever know that Willie had ventured out just before daybreak when he heard the search helicopters overhead. No one would know that when he came to the broken bridge he discovered Freddie lying against a tree where he had hit his head after being thrown from the bike. No one saw Strange Willie jump the

gorge on the motorcycle to rescue the boy. And no one was around as Strange Willie carried the boy in his arms back to the cabin where he wrapped him in the horse blanket. He trudged through the woods back to the broken bridge where he retrieved his motorcycle and was riding to get help when he was spotted by the police helicopter.

The whirring of its blades struck a forgotten nerve deep in Strange Willie's brain, and, before he realized it, the war veteran thought he was back in Vietnam pursued by the enemy. When he was taken into custody, his mind was so confused he had forgotten about the boy, and by the time it finally cleared, word had already reached search headquarters that the boy had been located, so there was nothing more for Strange Willie to say. Sitting in the back of the police cruiser, he curled up into his own silence. No one witnessed the single tear form in Strange Willie's eye as he watched the two whips usher Hampton into the back of the hound truck. When the door locked, Hampton whimpered as he sat alone on the bed of the cold pickup. The engine started and Strange Willie watched his friend driven off, perhaps never to be seen by him again. Strange Willie sank even deeper into himself. There was a rapping on the top of the cruiser and Sheriff Homestack opened the door signaling Willie to get out.

"Well, looks like the only thing you're guilty of is running away from trouble," the sheriff said. Strange Willie said nothing. He stared at the dirt and shuffled his feet, the sheriff's words not registering in his brain. He just wanted to be out of there. Carly watched from the doorway, trying to hear what the sheriff was saying. Some of the words were hard to understand from where she stood. Behind the cruiser, Monroe waited in grandfather's trailer. It looked to Carly as if Strange Willie were being reprimanded. She didn't understand why. Didn't they know that Willie had saved Freddie's life? She couldn't prove it, but something within told her that he was the real hero, a fact he would never acknowledge and no one would ever know.

"You know what, Willie? We don't like you hanging around. Bad things happen when you're here. Bad influence on the kids. I can't hold you on any formal charge, but I can strongly urge you to leave the area. Willie, it's what's best for you. Best for all of us. Besides, your trailer's burned to the ground. Nowhere for you to live. Been here too long anyway."

Willie didn't answer the sheriff. He kept looking at the ground. Carly darted from where she was standing and charged toward the sheriff.

"He didn't do anything. Leave him alone." Carly wailed angrily.

"Whoa, young lady. Nobody said he did anything. It's just time for him to be moving along. 'Sides, it's none of your concern. You and your young friend have caused quite enough trouble for one year," the sheriff scolded her.

Carly realized that the life of a hero was short-lived. Her grandfather took her by the hand and whisked her away from the sheriff back toward his red pickup truck. She turned toward Strange Willie, as he was escorted down the road on foot by the two state police officers. He never looked back. The snow turned to rain.

CHAPTER 25

Later that day, while Carly took a well-deserved afternoon nap, Walter Drury paid an unannounced visit. Although he frowned upon people who stopped by without notice, Grandpa Oakley was as gracious as ever as he welcomed the Hunt Master. The conversation from the living room awakened Carly who rested with Buster the cat curled at her side. Buster always welcomed a friend for afternoon siestas.

"Well, I wouldn't be too hard on her, Walter," she heard her grandfather say.

"What she did was wrong, Mather," Mr. Drury responded. "I know she's only eleven, but she does know right from wrong."

"You know better than I," her grandfather replied. "After all, it's been a while since I was a parent. Guess I've made a few mistakes second time around."

"You're doing a wonderful job. Don't be too hard on yourself," the visitor said, respectful of the circumstances under which Carly had come to the Oakley farm.

Carly appeared at the doorway wiping the sleep from her eyes. Buster stirred but refused to get up, although this unusual afternoon commotion aroused his curiosity.

"Good afternoon, Carly," Mr. Drury's baritone voice boomed through the farmhouse.

"Hello, sir." In contrast, Carly's voice was barely audible. "Is everything okay?"

"Mr. Drury would like to speak with you," said her grandfather.

Mr. Drury paced the rug in front of the couch where Carly now sat. Her grandfather stood behind the chair so that she could not see him directly.

"Carly, everyone in our community is very grateful for what you did this morning and your good deeds have not gone unnoticed." As he said this, an embarrassed smile crossed her lips. "But we can't overlook the fact that you knew where the missing hound was and yet you never told anyone."

Her smile disappeared as quickly as it had appeared. She stared at the rug. "I'm sorry, sir."

"You know Hampton is a very special hound. We put a lot of time, effort and money into the hounds and each one is very valuable to us. Your grandfather told me you knew for some time where to find Hampton. You know silence was just as wrong as telling a fib."

Carly sat in silence, thinking of Hampton, Strange Willie, and how the two had bonded. Her emotions were jumbled and, while she heard the words Mr. Drury spoke, she didn't know if what he was saying was true or not. He didn't have all the facts.

"But he saved Strange Willie's life," she started to say.

"Mr. Drury's right," her grandfather interrupted. "I think you owe him an apology."

"But Grandfather," she protested straightening her back.

“Nothing more to say, young lady,” he told her. “You owe the whole club an apology. They may never have gotten that hound back, no thanks to you.”

“This isn’t fair,” Carly cried. “I didn’t tell anybody about the hound because....”

“Now Carly,” her grandfather insisted, “Mr. Drury didn’t come here to hear excuses. A simple apology will do. Perhaps you’ll write a short note to the other members and staff of the Hunt.

Carly felt alone and wished her mother were here to help her through this difficult time. If this were what it’s like to be a hero, Strange Willie was right, she didn’t want anything more to do with it. Without further protest, she gave in to her grandfather's demands.

"I'm sorry, Mr. Drury," Carly said trying to convince them she was sincere. "I did a bad thing. I should have told you as soon as I found the missing hound. I hope I haven't caused too much trouble. It will never happen again."

"That's better, sweetheart," her grandfather nodded his approval.

"Fine, Carly. I accept your apology. I hope this has taught you a lesson. Good day, Mather. Good-bye Carly and give your pony an extra carrot tonight." Mr. Drury's voice turned friendly as he said good-bye leaving through the kitchen door. The rain changed back to snow and a light dusting of white covered the countryside. Mr. Drury's four-wheel drive truck left two distinct tracks in the snow as the Master headed home, satisfied that he had taught the young girl an important lesson in life.

That night Carly ate dinner in silence, not wishing to discuss the day's events with her grandfather. The phone rang incessantly, but the young lady refused everyone's calls. Her grandfather took messages of congratulations and passed them along to his granddaughter who acknowledged them through a nod of her head. Once in bed, she stared at the ceiling for many hours before finally falling asleep. Memories of the day's events flooded her brain. She was happy her friend had not been injured badly but wished the incident never happened.

"Grownups are the last to know anything," she said aloud to Buster, who was cleaning himself in the moonlight pouring through the window. He looked at her and yawned. Carly knew he understood what she was saying.

One thing seemed certain. She would never be invited to ride with the Hunt.

Oh well, she'd be moving far away when her parents returned in a few short months.

CHAPTER 26

Carly's return to school was mildly chaotic and the enthusiasm with which she was greeted caught the young girl off guard. Mr. Drury's words still stinging in her ears, Carly acted as if nothing special had happened. To her surprise she was swamped by her friends and the teachers, even the principal came by her classroom to shake her hand. Newspaper accounts of the search and rescue were posted on bulletin boards throughout the school and at lunch a videotape of a television news story featuring the young celebrity was broadcast to the classrooms. Her classmates constructed a huge get-well card for Freddie who was recovering at his home. He was expected back in school in several days. A rumor spread throughout the school that Monroe was on display at the gazebo in the center of town. These stories proved false. Carly accepted the praise of friends and even enjoyed the recognition by children and adults to whom she had never even spoken. It was a time of celebration, which lasted exactly twenty-four hours.

On her second day back at school, except for the bulletin boards, there was rarely any mention of the rescue. Carly slipped back into her role as a fifth grade student, although she did have more offers from kids who wanted to sit with her in the lunchroom. Her thoughts were never far from her friend, Freddie, and his brush with death and the mystery of how he ended up at the cabin.

On Wednesday, she was allowed to visit Freddie after school.

While the adults chatted in the kitchen eating Mrs. Wheeler's upside-down cake, Carly replayed the adventure for Freddie in his bedroom. He had been told how his best friend led the main search party that eventually found him, but this was the first time he heard first-hand her side of the story. He sat mesmerized as she recounted every detail of the rescue. Saddened by the news that Hampton had been returned to the kennel, Freddie was more curious about Strange Willie's disappearance. Nobody had mentioned his name to either child in the past few days and they could only speculate on his whereabouts. Carly and Freddie vowed to find Strange Willie when Freddie recovered, so he could tell them what really happened. In the meantime, she probed Freddie's memory trying to reconstruct any fragment of truth. Trying hard as he could, Freddie's memory of the accident remained locked tight. Not giving up, Carly tried to hypnotize her young friend, but all it did was make him hungry. The visit came to an abrupt end when Mrs. Wheeler and Grandpa Oakley returned from the kitchen.

"Time to go, Carly," grandfather said. "Freddie still needs lots of rest."

The friends said their good-byes and Carly promised she'd come back every afternoon. "I'll bring my homework, so you can keep up with schoolwork," she offered, looking for approval from her grandfather.

"If it's okay with Mrs. Wheeler?" he asked.

"Can she, mom?" pleaded Freddie.

"We'll see," said his mother, invoking her parental right to not answer questions directly.

Freddie returned to school the following Monday. Life in this semi-rural Virginia town marked time uneventfully. Monroe lost a shoe and Carly didn't ride him until the blacksmith nailed it back on. The pony didn't mind. Recent events had been much too exciting for him and he welcomed the rest.

Hampton didn't like being confined in the hound pen, although the food was ample and always served on time. The older hounds went on the regular hunts and from time to time several of the yearlings were chosen to join the pack. Hampton's name was never called. Perhaps they were afraid he would get lost again. Perhaps they thought he might run away. Perhaps they were right. Hampton sulked in a hound sort of way and took to sleeping most of the day. He wondered what happened to his friend with the loud motorcycle and would he see him or that funny red fox ever again?

CHAPTER 27

A light mist retreated from the valley, as the rising sun signaled the arrival of Thanksgiving morning, crisp and cool, a brilliant day across the Virginia countryside. Carly was excited as she raced through breakfast.

Buster the cat sniffed around the kitchen, overflowing with the smells of early turkey preparations. A delicious day awaited. For Carly this was to be a special Thanksgiving because Grandpa Oakley had promised they could ride out to the ridge and watch the Thanksgiving Hunt pass through the lower meadow. The holiday ride always attracted a huge hunt field, over one hundred riders, and, ever since moving in with her grandfather, Carly wanted to experience it up close. Despite being reprimanded by the Master, Carly was still enthralled with the Hunt. She knew that if Mr. Drury knew all the facts, he wouldn't have been angry with her. Oh well, that incident was weeks behind now and all was forgiven. She never gave up hope that someday she would ride with the Hunt.

While not actually participating in this day's event, Carly took extra care grooming Monroe, braiding his mane and polishing his hoofs to a high gloss. She was proud of her pony and wanted him to look his best. Grandpa Oakley rode Hardtack the mule. In fact, since riding with the search party, the old man had taken his old mule out for several recreational rides and was enjoying this leisure time, something farm work rarely allowed.

Dressed in her best white shirt, her father's old tweed jacket which he had worn in high school, her hair hanging in a ponytail from the back of her helmet, she and her grandfather set out for the ridge. The jacket was two sizes too big for Carly, but it made her feel as though she were wearing formal riding attire. She sat tall in the saddle and felt regal as the pony loped along, followed by her grandfather who was dressed less formally in traditional bib-style farmer overalls.

At the top of the ridge overlooking Muldair's Meadow, the pair was joined by several dozen other "hilltoppers," people who drove or walked to traditional viewpoints or checks.

Everyone enjoyed the spectacular view of the hunt passing below. On Thanksgiving Day, the ranks of the hilltoppers grew dramatically. Steaming coffee, doughnuts, and small cakes were passed around as the group waited. Somebody shared a thermos of hot chocolate with Carly. Monroe and Hardtack were quite content eating the abundant grass on the ridge.

The ridge provided terrific sight lines in three directions. From the east, the Hunt would burst out of a dense forest, charge over a brook and two low stone walls, followed by a challenging hand gallop through twenty acres of meadow interrupted by four ancient stone walls. Completing the picture and framing the west side was a railroad trestle that spanned a small river. Fifty yards to the left of the trestle, the river naturally narrowed permitting a shallow crossing for the hounds and horses.

Warmed by her hot chocolate, Carly tuned her senses to hear the first faint baying of the distant hounds. Monroe knew before anyone, lifting his head from his eating, flicking his right ear in the direction of the approaching hounds. What a glorious sight as the field of riders came into view, painting a streak of colors across the landscape. Carly watched through her grandfather's binoculars, making her feel right in the middle of the action. She felt every pounding hoof step, glided over every jump, and larked with the riders as they careened across the glen.

Carly focused the binoculars on Mr. Drury in the lead as he skillfully maneuvered over obstacles, his horse powerful and balanced in his soft hands. In the distance the lonely whistle of an Amtrak passenger train echoed in the hills. She thought little of the warning signal having heard trains on a regular basis as they passed safely through the valley. As Carly watched, something terrible happened. In full stride O'Toole, the Master's fiery Irish hunter, stepped in a hidden woodchuck hole, stumbled, and sent Mr. Drury crashing with a thud in the tall, soft meadow grass. All around him, staff and field members rushed to his side, while the hounds continued their frantic pace, pushing further away from the fallen Master.

Brushing himself off, the uninjured Master yelled at his whips. "Don't bother with me. Get after the hounds. The river crossing is coming. Go catch them." Seeing that his valued hunter was not injured, he remounted.

Putting down the binoculars, Carly refocused on the panoramic view.

Besides Mr. Drury's fall, something else was wrong. She sensed the danger although she couldn't pinpoint exactly what it was. Then it struck her. The whistle! The hounds, which were now a half-mile in front of the nearest whip, were following the fox scent right into trouble. Instead of taking the shallow river crossing, the hounds jumped onto the railroad tracks and were about to cross the river on the railroad trestle. Not noticed by anyone, the Silver Comet, an Amtrak passenger train carrying one-hundred-and-eighty unwary passengers, was rapidly approaching the trestle from the opposite direction.

Carly and the hilltoppers sensed the impending danger, as the first hound hopped onto the steel span and headed across the trestle, jumping from one railroad tie to the next. They were too far away to warn the hounds. At the speed the train was approaching, it would be on top of the unsuspecting animals before they could be called off the trestle by whips, still far away.

Carly first caught sight of it out of the corner of her eye, a glint of sunshine reflecting off a mirror-like surface. She squinted and tried to focus on the speeding object, unsure at first what it was. As it became clear to her, she excitedly pointed toward a speeding rider. There was no doubt. Carly saw Strange Willie flying at eighty miles an hour toward the trestle and the endangered hounds. He was riding on the rail bed parallel to the tracks some three hundred yards in front of the speeding passenger train. And as he rode toward the river, the faster train slowly gained ground on him. As the train bore down on the fearless motorcycle rider, the engineer blew his whistle.

Ignoring the warning, Strange Willie increased his speed and like a stunt rider jumped onto the tracks riding directly in front of the Silver Comet. Realizing something was wrong, the engineer applied the brakes and a scream of rushing air billowed out. The brakes tried to hold back the tonnage of onrushing railroad cars. Strange Willie kept pushing forward, his head bent low toward the handlebars, ignoring the imminent danger.

Thump...thump...thump. Every bump of his wheels against the railroad ties jolted his whole body as he rode over the trestle. Oblivious to the danger, the preoccupied hounds were nearly halfway across the trestle when they finally heard the screech-

ing train brakes and looked up to see the motorcycle and Strange Willie fast approaching. The huge silver engine loomed ominously in the background as it continued its slide toward the railroad bridge. Strange Willie screamed at the top of his lungs and waved his one free hand. Closing in, Mr. Drury caught up to the pack and with a blast of his hunt horn called the hounds back. Heeding the warning, the hounds turned heel and ran off the bridge to safety. Strange Willie gunned his motorcycle engine and flew by the astonished field that was watching just below the trestle. The Amtrak lumbered to a stop halfway across the bridge, right at the spot where the lead hound had been seconds earlier. A few more yards and the pack of frantic hounds would have been crushed.

Cheers cascaded from the hilltop where the people heralded Strange Willie's heroic deed. Carly and her Grandfather remounted and headed down the hill toward the Hunt. She hoped Strange Willie would stop and come back, but the only trace of the man was a cloud of dust his motorcycle left as it sped out of view down an old tractor road. Mr. Drury stepped from his horse and called the hounds to his side. He was visibly shaken. His gaze rose from the ground as he looked down the road at the distant motorcycle rider, before turning his attention toward Carly and her grandfather as they approached the stunned riders. He smiled at the young girl then turned to remount his horse. No words were exchanged.

CHAPTER 28

Later that afternoon, Carly had plenty to be thankful for as she joined her grandfather, Freddie, and Mrs. Wheeler for Thanksgiving dinner at the Oakley farm. She and Freddie cleared the table, preparing for pumpkin pie. A loud rumble outside sent chickens scurrying, while Monroe and Hardtack paced nervously in their stalls. Dashing to the window, Carly saw Strange Willie riding down the drive, trailing smoke and dust. As the entire Thanksgiving party rushed for the front porch, she stopped them with a wave of her hand.

"Let me go alone," she pleaded. No one disagreed. Carly ventured onto the porch. Strange Willie turned the engine off and waited silently as the girl approached. He held a blackened tin box in his hand.

"Hi, Willie," Carly smiled. He returned a nod but spoke no words.

"You're a real hero."

After a few awkward seconds he spoke. "Don't want to be no hero," said the tattered man, looking at the ground.

"But you are, and the people around here want to thank you, personally," Carly persisted.

"Don't want no people thanking me. Sides, nobody wants me around."

"That's not true, Willie," she said. "After what you did today, I'm sure they'd make you an honorary member of the Hunt."

"Don't want to be a hero," he repeated. "Just want my dawg back." He spoke the last words so softly Carly had to ask him to repeat himself.

"Can you get me my dawg, back?" Strange Willie asked again.

"I don't know if I can or not, but I can sure ask," Carly assured him.

"Would appreciate that," he said humbly, looking up as

Mrs. Wheeler came out onto the porch. She carried a brown paper bag and whispered in Carly's ear as she handed it to her, then disappeared back into the house, where she watched through the window along with Grandpa Oakley and Freddie.

"I suppose you haven't had your Thanksgiving dinner?"

Carly asked, as she handed him the brown paper bag, which held two turkey sandwiches.

Strange Willie took the offering and stuffed it into his torn jacket.

"Did you rescue, Freddie?" Carly asked, knowing she might never get another opportunity to solve the puzzle.

"Don't know nothing about rescuing Freddie," Strange Willie lied as he winked at Carly. "Just want my dawg back." The way he spoke assured Carly that Willie had been the hero that day also. She knew he wouldn't say any more. It was good enough for her. She had the answer she wanted. She didn't need more words to solve the mystery.

"I'll do my best, " Carly said. "Where can I find you?"

"I'll find you," he answered. Returning to the motorcycle, he revved the engine and was off down the winding driveway without saying good-bye. Willie raised his hand and waved as he rode off.

CHAPTER 29

Later Thanksgiving evening, Carly and her grandfather drove to Mr. Drury's sprawling mansion on a hill a dozen miles away. He and 15 members of the Hunt greeted the farmer and his granddaughter as they arrived in the old red pickup truck. Heartfelt handshakes were exchanged and in animated conversation the group recounted the strange events of the day. Everyone wanted to find Strange Willie and parade him through the town as a hero. Above the commotion, the voice of the young girl quieted the group.

"Willie doesn't want to be a hero," she spoke in clear strong tones. "He just wants to be left alone. What he did was nothing special to Willie. He was just doing what Willie does." She turned to Mr. Drury. "Willie did have one request. He wants to know if you could return Hampton to him."

Mr. Drury hesitated before speaking. "Carly, that's not such an outlandish request," he said to the amazement of the other guests. "You know, some hounds are outstanding citizens and make good pack members, while others are meant to be pets. And after what Strange Willie did for all of us today, I think it can be arranged," he continued. "After all, it's a small price to pay for saving the entire pack." Then he turned to the hunt members gathered around him. "Well, if we can't find this man to thank him in person, let's give him a rousing Riverdale Hunt cheer. To Willie. Hip, hip, hooray."

The celebration continued as guests one by one toasted Willie, their reluctant, silent hero. Mr. Drury invited Carly to join the Hunt as a junior member. Carly hugged her grandfather.

Later that Thanksgiving night, she returned to the farm in the red pick-up truck, Hampton sitting on the front seat between her grandfather and herself.

CHAPTER 30

Two days later as Carly sat with Hampton on her front porch wondering when Strange Willie would return, she noticed the small blackened tin tucked under a porch railing. She carefully pried open the tin, revealing its contents, an unscarred gold locket. Inside the locket Carly found a tiny photograph of a handsome proud soldier in full dress uniform. She closed the locket and turning it over, discovered a simple message engraved on the back "With Love, William, 1967."

Late that afternoon Strange Willie returned for his 'dawg'. No one could tell who was more excited, Strange Willie or Hampton. And as he slowly rode away with Hampton trotting by his side, only Carly saw the red fox peeking for an instant from the saddlebag on his motorcycle.

BILL MILLER has been riding to the hounds for over 40 years. For nearly 20 years he has been an honorary whipper-in for the Norfolk Hunt Club. Bill is also actively involved in Team Penning during the summer months. He lives on a small farm in Sherborn, Massachusetts with his wife and three horses. When not working with horses, Bill is an independent film director and cinematographer. His website is: www.billmillerfilm.com

MARY BURKHARDT is an artist whose illustrations have been included in a wide variety of both text and trade books during her long career in educational publishing. Now retired in Ithaca, New York with her husband Al, she is happily spending much of her time painting portraits of two of her favorite subjects, children and dogs.

AL BURKHARDT has been a book designer for many years in New York and California. He is now retired in Ithaca with his wife Mary where he enjoys painting and computer art.

Made in the USA
Charleston, SC
11 November 2010